# Lover's Quarrel

I couldn't resist getting on Stanley's case about picking such a terrible guy to take Thelma out.

"I hardly knew him," Stanley protested. "You said the other guy was too young. So I see this guy and I think, *This is who I should have fixed Thelma up with.* Then I heard he was looking for a date for this bash, and I thought it was destiny or something."

"Destiny! She figures her life is ruined and she's permanently mad at me. Sometimes I wonder where your brains are."

Stanley is not a person you can push too far, and apparently I was doing it.

"This whole quarter, you've been on my case," he said. "Forcing me to go to those parties when I didn't want to, getting me to fix up your unhappy friend, and then complaining about how it turns out. You're never satisfied. Sometimes I wonder how I ever got mixed up with you in the first place. I've had enough, and since you keep wanting to change me, I guess you've had enough of me, too. We better just forget about each other.

I was totally speechless. Forget about Stanley!

**Books by Emily Hallin**

Partners
Changes
Risks

Available from ARCHWAY Paperbacks

# *Risks*

**EMILY HALLIN**

A
Meg
And
Stanley
Story

**AN ARCHWAY PAPERBACK**
Published by POCKET BOOKS

New York   London   Toronto   Sydney   Tokyo   Singapore

This book is a work of fiction. Names, characters, places and incidents are either the product of the author's imagination or are used fictitiously. Any resemblance to actual events or locales or persons, living or dead, is entirely coincidental.

AN ARCHWAY PAPERBACK *Original*

An Archway Paperback published by
POCKET BOOKS, a division of Simon & Schuster Inc.
1230 Avenue of the Americas, New York, NY 10020

ISBN: 0-671-70589-X

First Archway Paperback printing July 1990

10 9 8 7 6 5 4 3 2 1

AN ARCHWAY PAPERBACK and colophon are registered trademarks of Simon & Schuster Inc.

Printed in the U.S.A.

IL 6+

*to Dave*

# Risks

**1**

DAPHNE WAINWRIGHT CORNERED ME when I arrived for my candy stripers shift at Hillview Hospital on Saturday afternoon. Her usually milk-white complexion was flushed with a glow of pink. I knew she was excited about something.

"I did it," she said.

"You did what?" I asked.

"I asked Kent Whitehead out."

"But doesn't he still have his broken leg?"

"He's got a walking cast now. Of course, he still limps. But I couldn't wait. I told him that he'd been sitting home alone long enough and he deserved to have some fun. I offered to go over and pick him up on Sunday night and take him out."

"How nice!" I said, laughing. "A candy striper who doesn't let her concern and care for patients stop at the hospital."

"Not when it's Kent Whitehead, that foxy jock."

I gave Daphne a narrow-eyed look. If there was anything Kent Whitehead wasn't, in my opinion, it was foxy. Daphne, the glamorous debutante, had fallen for Kent when he'd been in the hospital, a local high school basketball star wounded in action. Although I considered him boring, she thought he was the strong, silent jock type. I think she idealized him because she went to a girls' school, Crystal Creek, and had always wanted to go with someone from a public high school.

"The only thing is," she said, "now that he's said he'll go out with me, I don't know where to take him. I've never asked anyone out before. All the times I've been out with guys, they've asked me, and they've planned everything."

"All guys like to eat," I suggested. "Take him to Papa's Pizza."

"That's too crowded and noisy. I thought of something more private. Another thing," she added, "I'm afraid I won't be fun enough for him. I wish we could double-date. I was wondering if you and Stanley might—"

"Oh, sorry," I said. "Stanley and I promised to go

2

to my friend Lee Ann Adams's on Sunday night. Besides, you don't have to worry about entertaining Kent. I could tell the minute he met you he was knocked out by you. All you have to do is be your beautiful self."

Daphne has this long, cascading golden hair and gigantic dark blue eyes. Her facial structure is unbelievable. She was the star of the debutante cotillion last winter. (I only heard, I wasn't there.) She's probably the most poised person I know. So it was almost silly to hear her say that she might lose her confidence around Kent Whitehead. Kent has got to be the worst bumpkin at Hillview High, where we go to school. I've known him since grade school, and some of the most painful hours of my life have been spent trying to pry conversation out of Kent.

Anyway, Daphne had this incredible crush on Kent. Since I had introduced them at the hospital, what could I do but try to understand her infatuation with Kent?

"I'm serious, Meg. I need help. Kent is from a different world. I'm afraid I'll feel out of it around him. I know you'll think I'm pushy, but maybe if Kent and I could go to your friend's with you? I know it's asking a lot, but . . ."

Daphne had been a good friend to me. She had helped get me in good with the mother of Stanley Stoneman, my heartthrob for life. I owed her a favor in return, but I didn't want to wreck Lee Ann's party.

3

"I don't know what to say. If it were my party, sure, you and Kent would be more than welcome. But it's at Lee Ann's. She's just having three couples, but maybe I could persuade her to squeeze in one more. I'll ask and let you know."

"You're great, Meg Royce," Daphne said. "I'll keep my fingers crossed."

Lee Ann wasn't too receptive to the idea. "The whole purpose of this party is to get our trio together with our boyfriends," she reminded me. "It won't be the same with strangers around. We were going to see if the three of us could have as much fun with boys as we had before we started dating. Remember?"

"Daphne isn't exactly a stranger, and neither is Kent. Daphne's a friend of Stanley's, mine, and Kent's—and everybody knows Kent. Thelma even thought of dating him before she started going with Cory."

Lee Ann frowned. "She's not exactly going with Cory. The truth is, he's never asked her out. She's done all the asking. But—oh, well, why not? Tell Daphne okay. Only this is a potluck, so tell her and Kent they have to bring something."

"I'm sure Daphne will be glad to. She'll be so grateful. This is her first date with Kent, and she feels that she needs some moral support."

"Why is it people always come to you for advice and help, Meg?" Lee Ann asked.

"I can't figure that out, myself," I said.

Stanley Stoneman, my boyfriend and date for Lee Ann's potluck, is no party animal. I almost needed help myself to persuade him to go with me. What he likes to do best is hang out in a lab or metal shop and work on weird inventions, with me as an audience.

Sunday afternoon Daphne called to ask if she and Kent could go over to Lee Ann's with Stanley and me. "I'd feel so out of it just appearing at a stranger's door, but if we went with you and Stanley, that would make it okay," she said.

I was beginning to wish the party had never been organized. I didn't have time to tell Stanley that Daphne and Kent were going with us. When he came for me, I was still working on the salad that was my contribution to dinner. Stanley brought a long loaf of French bread.

Stanley was chopping celery for me when Daphne and Kent arrived. Kent stumbled into the house on his crutches, and Stanley looked astonished when he saw the strange pair.

"Oh," I explained. "I forgot to tell you that Daphne and Kent are driving over with us."

A bewildered expression spread over Stanley's face, but he didn't say anything.

"I'll drive," Daphne said. She must have noticed Stanley's car sitting out in front. It's a weird concoction of nuts, bolts, and sheet metal. Even though Stanley is from the richest family in town, he made and drives his own car because he's so creative.

"Okay," I agreed quickly, knowing there wouldn't be room for Daphne and Kent in Stanley's car. I glanced out of the corner of my eye at Stanley's gathering frown. I knew he didn't like the idea of driving with Daphne.

In case you don't know Daphne and Stanley's history together, I'd better bring you up-to-date. I first met Stanley at a ballroom dancing class. He was taking lessons because he had to escort Daphne to her debutante cotillion. But they didn't become a couple —we did. Stanley and I stayed partners even after dance class was over. Daphne and I became friends working with the candy stripers, the high school girls who volunteer at the hospital.

I guess Stanley was miffed at Daphne's horning in on my Hillview High crowd, when she had her own friends out at Crystal Creek, her posh private girls' school. He was also miffed at Kent Whitehead. He resented Kent because I had asked Kent to take me to my grandparents' anniversary party.

So, as you can see, our double date didn't start out terrifically.

"I had our cook make up one of her fantastic chicken and artichoke casseroles," Daphne said. "It'll go great with your salad."

"Should I have brought something?" Kent asked.

"You're excused," Daphne said flirtatiously. "Nobody expects you to cook when you're in a cast."

When the salad was finished and we were all

trooping out to get into Daphne's car, Stanley gave me a reproachful look. He was too polite to ask me about Daphne and Kent in their presence, but when we arrived at Lee Ann's, he took me aside instantly and asked, "How did Daphne get into this group? I thought it was just your old girlfriends."

I explained what had happened, and he made a disgusted face. "She has her own crowd. Why does she have to intrude on yours?"

"Come on, Stanley. Daphne has been a good friend of mine. Remember, she helped me get in good with your mother."

"And what's she doing with Kent Whitehead, that tongue-tied creep? Isn't there any limit to guys she'll add to her list?"

"Stanley! It's not like you to say mean things about people. She really likes Kent. She says he's a relief after that blabbermouth, Sonny Whitlow. I was looking forward to spending tonight with you. Let's not spoil it, okay?"

"Okay, Meg. I'm sorry, but just remember I'm not a social butterfly." We were in a fairly private place, and he made things all right by hugging me and snatching a quick kiss.

"Let's just let Daphne and Kent take care of themselves," I said.

We went in to say hi to everyone else. Lee Ann's date, Brian Hotchkiss, who was an oboe player in the school orchestra, had just arrived. I had only seen him

7

a couple of times at school, but I understood why Lee Ann had fallen for him. He was a happy-looking, slightly short guy with blond curly hair. He walked in a springy way like a confident elf. He grinned at Stanley. "So this is Stan and Meg. I keep hearing about you," he said.

The last to come were Thelma Arkadian and Cory Watkins, screeching into Lee Ann's driveway in Cory's Bronco.

After Cory had been introduced to Stanley and me, Cory asked Thelma, "What am I supposed to shoot?"

Embarrassment colored Thelma's face, and I instantly got the picture. In order to get a date with Cory, she'd told him they were going to take pictures of this party for the school paper. Cory was a tall, sandy-haired guy with a crafty face. When he looked at me, I felt that his calculating eyes were siphoning off my innermost secrets. The slightly amused smile that flickered around the corners of his mouth gave me the feeling that he found me a bit ridiculous.

Daphne had settled Kent on the patio and came back into the house to get him a soft drink. Cory watched in speechless wonder as Daphne floated gracefully through the room in a short skirt and a striped tank top. He seemed bowled over by her long, slender legs and model's figure. His eyes widened as he took in the incredible bone structure of her face. The backlighting from the patio etched the cascading waves of her hair with golden highlights, giving her an angelic look.

8

"Hey, just stand there, whoever you are. Don't move!"

Cory took the lens cover off his camera and focused. The camera clicked and whirred several times as he shot Daphne from different angles.

"You've worked as a model before," he stated, letting the camera flop from a strap around his neck.

"No, honestly!" Daphne took on an appealing air of bewilderment. "What's happening, anyway?"

"You're about to become famous, is what," Cory said with a big smile. "See, I'm the photographer for our school paper where your picture will be in the next issue."

I could see that Thelma's spirits were hitting the floor, that she wished she could be any place except right there.

"Her picture shouldn't wind up in our school paper. She doesn't go to our school," Stanley told Cory abruptly.

"That explains it," Cory said. "I thought I'd never seen anything like her at Hillview High."

Daphne looked cool. "Excuse me. I promised Kent a Coke," she said, squeezing between Stanley and Cory and walking into the kitchen.

Stanley shot me a look. I knew he was waiting until we were alone to remind me that having Daphne at the party was risky.

Brian Hotchkiss wasn't immune to Daphne's charms, either. He sort of showed off for her benefit, clowning and telling jokes in a louder than usual voice. Lee Ann became reserved and wary. This party was going nowhere. It was all my fault for telling Daphne she could come.

When Daphne passed us again on her way outside with Kent's Coke, Cory cornered her. "We could use you as a model down at Teen Togs at the mall. I take pictures every month for their ad in the school paper. You'd have to wear one of the dresses featured in the ad. I'll suggest you to the owner. I know she'll say yes, especially when she sees you. You're interested, aren't you? You'd be a natural."

Thelma was glowering. My uneasiness increased.

"I'll think about it." Daphne disappeared through the patio door.

"Why don't we all go out there?" Cory suggested, and everyone wandered out to the patio. Everyone except Stanley, that is. He had spotted a telescope on an upstairs landing and escaped from us by climbing the stairs and looking into space. When the rest of us were outside, Lee Ann said she'd get out the volleyball net and we could have a game.

"But Kent can't play," Daphne objected.

Lee Ann has the sunniest disposition I know, but I caught an angry glance moving from her to Daphne. It was as if she were saying, "This is my yard and my party, so I'll decide what we're going to do."

I racked my brain for a way to save the day, especially for Thelma. I suggested we play Trivial Pursuit. Thelma is supersmart. She gets good grades and reads a lot, and I had a feeling she'd be the star of the game.

In fact, it turned out to be a good game for everyone. Stanley, after scanning the neighborhood with the telescope, wandered out to join us. He knew all the answers to the scientific questions. Lee Ann and Brian were unstoppable on music. Kent chimed in with answers to the sports questions, and the rest of us contributed with general knowledge. Daphne had never played the game before.

"I'm getting myself a set," she said.

After the game all the guys' eyes, except for Stanley's, settled on Daphne again. I'm famous as a chatterbox, so I did what I could to get the attention on someone besides my gorgeous debutante friend.

"Lee Ann and Brian," I said. "Tell us how your plans for going to Tokyo are working out."

"Mr. Giacomo got us some little Japanese phrase books. We're learning a little of the language," Brian said. "For instance, *Wakarimasen.*"

"Sounds complicated," Stanley said. "What's it mean?"

"It means, 'I don't understand,'" Lee Ann said. "Here's another: *Dozo yoh roh sheeku.*"

"Meaning, 'I'm glad to meet you,'" Brian said. "Here's another: *Nanji deska.*"

"That's 'What time is it?'" Lee Ann said.

They went through the Japanese numbers from one to ten. Then they told about other preparations they were making to go to Tokyo in the summer with the high school orchestra.

"We never do anything outrageous like that at Crystal Creek," Daphne complained. "Our school is too small. We'd never have enough kids for an orchestra large enough to take overseas."

"How about a paper? You do have one of those, don't you?" Cory asked.

Daphne shrugged. "We have one, but it's a sleazy little mimeographed sheet. Anybody in school can write for it, but if it's gossip or a complaint about the school operations, it gets zapped out. Our headmistress censors everything."

"A dictatorship," Thelma commented.

"Yeah," Brian added. "You need freedom of speech at your school."

Attention had again focused on Daphne. I tried to deflect it to Thelma, and to pair her up with Cory. "Cory and Thelma are on our school paper. They're quite a team. With Thelma's dynamic prose and Cory's fantastic photos, they make the Hillview *Howl* a real page-turner," I said.

"The big things at Hillview this quarter are the track meet, the student body elections, and the science fair for all the area high schools," Thelma said.

"Our track meet is called Field Day," Daphne said. "It's not worth the trouble. As for the science fair, a couple of girls in our school are scientific types and they'll enter, but our school won't even have its own section."

12

"There's a lot of competition at our school; everyone tries to get a project in the fair for extra credit, but we all know who'll win: Stanley," I said.

Stanley looked down at the ground. He didn't like to be in the spotlight, and Cory, who'd been staring boldly at Daphne, turned it back on her.

"A picture is worth a thousand words," he said almost to himself. "Especially a picture of you."

Kent rose from his chair and tottered on his walking cast toward Cory, challenging him. He opened his mouth, but no words came out.

Stanley raked his hand through his wavy dark hair and gave me an I-told-you-so look.

Thelma sort of shrunk inside herself. She was at a total disadvantage. A wiry, olive-skinned girl whose dark hair was wild and hard to manage, she gave the impression of being a studious type. Thelma's attractiveness came from her energy and animation. When she was thinking up something fun or unusual to do, her dark eyes flashed and a glow radiated beneath her swarthy skin. But Cory had quenched her creative spirit then. She was going to be a dud for the rest of the party.

She only picked at her dinner, hardly eating at all. I made a point of sitting next to her and keeping up a conversation with her because Cory acted as if he hadn't come with her at all. He flitted around shooting pictures—mostly of Daphne.

When we'd finished eating, he said, "Sorry to eat and run, kids, but I want to see how these shots came

13

out." He turned to Daphne. "I'll see you get a set." Then he was gone.

Thelma disappeared into Lee Ann's room. I followed her to see if she was okay.

She was about to cry. "It's pretty obvious that Cory wasn't a real date, isn't it?" she said angrily. "I told him Miss Wagstaff had suggested we cover a story about what Hillview kids do on the weekend. I thought he'd at least stay till the end."

"That egotistical dork!" I said.

"He didn't even care that he'd driven me over and left me stranded."

I started to say that she could ride home with Stanley and me when I remembered that Daphne was driving.

After Thelma and I went back to the party, Stanley seemed to be conscious of Thelma's situation. He's that kind of a sensitive guy.

"Hey, it's such a nice evening," he said. "Why don't we walk home? It's not that far. Feel like some exercise, Thelma?"

"I was thinking that same thing," Thelma said. We made excuses to Daphne and Kent, and took off for my house.

After Thelma peeled off at the corner, I expected Stanley to say he'd warned me about having Daphne, but he didn't say a thing. In fact, he didn't say much on the rest of the way home except, "Wow, I'm glad that's over! Face it, Meg, I'll never be a party guy."

His old jalopy was sitting in front of my house, and

he headed straight for it, hoisting himself in. I ran to the car to claim a good night kiss, which turned out to be an unsatisfactory peck.

"See ya," he said, driving away.

Were my efforts to change Stanley into a more social type turning him off?

# 2 ➤

DAPHNE PHONED THE NEXT DAY after school. "That was a terrific party," she said. "Kent loved it, too. In fact, I had so much fun that I'd like to get everyone together at my house next Sunday, sort of to make up for crashing that party. You could either give me their phone numbers or you could invite them for me."

I had an uneasy feeling that another disaster was brewing. "I see them all the time at school," I said quickly. "I could do the inviting and let you know who can come."

"Great. Keep me posted. I already told Kent about it and he said he'd be there. He could help you call, maybe phone the guys."

"He needn't bother. I'll do it all." I planned to omit an invitation to Cory. I knew I'd have a gigantic task persuading Stanley to come for a repeat performance of something he hadn't wanted to do in the first place. I knew he'd feel that he was being forced back into the social scene he'd been trying to avoid all his life.

Life had been so simple for me and my friends before boys came into it. Thelma, Lee Ann, and I had been content just to hang out. Now we were all mixed up, but we could never go back to the way we'd been last year. At least two of us couldn't. Lee Ann wouldn't be satisfied without Brian, and I could never be happy again without Stanley's company. But Thelma hadn't found a boyfriend, and that seemed to put a strain on our friendship.

Another thing that complicated life was that Stanley wasn't too fond of associating with people. He just wanted the two of us to hole up and work on his scientific experiments, and he resisted my efforts to socialize him. I wasn't trying to push him into high-powered social events like debutante balls and country club dinners. But I thought a little informal gathering with a few friends would give him a break from his intense intellectual activity once in a while.

The next day between classes I brought up Daphne's party after Stanley explained something he'd just done in physics.

"Daphne wants to pay us back for taking her and Kent to Lee Ann's," I said. "She's invited us over

Sunday for dinner. Kent is going, and so are Lee Ann and Brian. Maybe Thelma."

Stanley's amazement was total. He couldn't even speak for a moment. "I can't believe someone would want to repeat that fiasco!" he exclaimed. "You're not serious."

"Daphne didn't think it was a fiasco. She had a blast."

"She would. She had all the guys hanging around her as usual. Why can't she be satisfied with Sonny Whitlow?"

We both looked at each other and burst out laughing.

"What I mean is, why does she have to horn in on you and me, Meg?"

"You're just prejudiced against Daphne because her parents know your parents. She never says rotten things about you, and give her credit for discovering that Sonny is a jerk. Give her a break! She's just being friendly, which is something you never bother with. Daphne is trying to escape from the same social scene you did, to get to know new people. You ought to understand and help. Say you'll go, please."

Stanley looked offended.

"I wasn't putting you down," I explained hastily. "One of the best things about you is the way you insist on being your own person. There's nobody in the world like you—as wonderful as you. Only you should mix with other people once in a while."

"I'm starting to bore you," he said accusingly. He peered into my eyes to see if I agreed.

"Never!" In spite of the crowds in the hallway, I gave him a hug. "You're the most exciting guy in the whole town of Hillview. Maybe in California, as far as I know."

"Then why wreck the combination of you and me by going to some stupid party?"

"If you're there, it won't be stupid." I made little finger tracks around the back of his ear, which made him smile.

"Maybe just this once," he said. "But this is the last time."

Although I had told Stanley that Lee Ann and Brian were coming, I hadn't asked them yet. When I did, they didn't have to be wheedled.

"Wow!" Lee Ann exclaimed. "I never thought I'd be asked to a party in a mansion!"

Brian thought it would be awesome, too. "I'll bring my trick cards."

Lee Ann made a face. "Please don't. And don't bring along any of your other tacky tricks, either."

She turned to me. "Brian has been haunting the joke store," she said. "He has a whole collection of gags: whoopee cushion, dribble glass, ink spot, cotton doughnuts, plastic dog doo, and all that."

"It gets a lot of laughs out of the guys in the orchestra," Brian said.

"*Some* of them," Lee Ann amended. "The victims aren't always amused."

19

"If they're good sports, they are."

"You and Brian work that out. Anyway, you'll come?"

"With bells on," Brian said.

"You bet," Lee Ann added.

There was just Thelma to ask now. Without a boyfriend, Thelma might feel awkward about going, so I hesitated to invite her.

I called Daphne to tell her that Stanley and I, and Lee Ann and Brian, accepted the invitation, but that Cory and Thelma had broken up. "Thelma might come, but we better leave Cory out," I said.

"It's just as well, since I don't want him to nag me about modeling for that dress shop, which my mother says I can't do."

"I'm afraid Thelma won't want to come without a date."

"No date!" This seemed unbelievable to Daphne. After a few moments of shocked silence, she recovered. "No problem," she said. "I'll just get Wally Urquhart to come over. He lives next door. He's fairly okay, and he's always available. So tell Thelma a date will be furnished."

Even so, I wasn't sure Thelma would be willing to mix with the same group that had seen her dumped by Cory, or that she'd care to see Daphne again.

"Are you kidding!" she exclaimed in an outraged tone when I told her she was invited to Daphne's. "After she broke Cory and me up?"

"She wasn't responsible. It was Cory," I told her. "Daphne didn't pay any attention to Cory. She was too concerned about Kent. She probably didn't even realize you came with him. She might have thought you were Brian's date, or that everyone just came alone.

"Anyway, Thelma, she kind of needs you there, because there's an extra guy coming, Wally someone, and she thought you and he might hit it off."

Thelma looked startled and then thoughtful. "Wally who?"

"I can't pronounce his last name."

"I don't know any Wallys at school."

"He doesn't go to Hillview. He's from Broxton Academy."

"Oh?" Thelma looked interested. Broxton was an exclusive boys' school attended by rich guys. Although Stanley considered it a stuffy place, many Hillview kids thought it was glamorous because it was expensive.

"He's from a wealthy family, like Stanley, right?"

"Wealthy, maybe, but not necessarily like Stanley."

"Oh, well, if they need a date for this extra guy . . ." Curiosity was getting the better of Thelma.

"Wally lives next door to Daphne, so he'll already be there. You can ride over with Stanley and me."

"I don't want to butt in on your date."

"You're not butting in. I invited you. It'll be fun to have you with us."

Thelma looked skeptical. "You're just trying to make me feel good. It's too embarrassing to go without a date, so count me out."

I had to wheedle and reason with her for a little while longer before she finally agreed to come.

It was a good thing I had Thelma to talk to on the way to Daphne's because Stanley was so grossed out at having to attend another social function that he wasn't saying much.

"What's happening at the *Howl?*" I asked Thelma.

"I've been knocking myself out doing extra assignments and also taking on other people's work when they goof off," Thelma said. "I'm determined to be editor of the paper next year. Wanda Zetterquist also wants it, and so does Turner Spivey. Could you imagine the paper with Wanda as editor? All gossip and rumors. And with that egghead, Turner, it would be totally boring."

"I'll vote for you," Stanley said. "It sounds like a clear choice."

"Unfortunately, nobody votes for the school paper editor," Thelma said. "Miss Wagstaff just assigns somebody toward the end of spring quarter. That's why I'm trying so hard to make an impression on her. I need to have some outstanding extracurricular activity to get a scholarship next year when I apply for college. We already have two in college, and that's all my dad and mom can stand."

"You ought to get it if you're doing all the work," Stanley said. "Well, here we are. I'll let you ladies out and park the car." He had pulled into the circular drive.

"Do I look okay?" Thelma viewed the Wainwright mansion warily. It had pillars in front like Tara in *Gone with the Wind.*

"Sure, great," I assured her, although I thought she was too dressed up. She had borrowed a glittery sweater from her oldest sister. Stanley was only wearing a sports shirt, and he knew what they wore in this neighborhood.

Kent was already there, and he was in a coat and tie. All the confusion about what to wear was the result of kids from the posh side of town mixing with ordinary kids like us.

I could hear Thelma's awe in the loud way she drew in her breath when we entered the Wainwrights' marble entry hall with the curving staircase. Descending it, gorgeous as usual, her golden hair flowing over her shoulders, was Daphne, in a blue jumpsuit.

"Oh, Meg, how great to see you." Daphne sped down the staircase and gave me a hug. "And Thelma! I'm glad you could come. Kent! You're already here! Did I keep you waiting? Let's all go in the parlor. We don't want Kent standing on that leg too long."

Brian and Lee Ann arrived a few minutes later. Brian always wore an eager expression, which matched his manner of plunging forward on his high-arched feet. Lee Ann kept peering around the elaborately furnished room, as if she were sneaking a peek at things she wasn't allowed to see.

The last to arrive was Wally Urquhart, a very tall, thin guy with dark, unruly hair and the kind of very thick glasses that magnify a person's eyes.

I glanced at Thelma, who was dying of embarrassment. I could tell she wished a creature with a magic wand would come and whisk her out of this setting and back home. I put myself in her place. I'd feel the same way if suddenly I was confronted by a stranger who was supposed to be my date. Wally was carrying a tennis racket and was dressed all in white.

When Daphne introduced him around the room, he repeated several times that he was sorry to be so rumpled, but he'd just been in a tournament. When he came to me, he said hopefully, "Oh, are you my date?"

Daphne said, "She's Stoneman's. Remember, you met her before at the country club."

"We danced together," I said reproachfully.

"How could I forget?" he said, which drew a scowl from Stanley.

As I said before, the attractive part of Thelma is her liveliness. She likes to organize things. When she's in the middle of getting people to go on a picnic or have a car wash or garage sale to save the whales or something, she's a ball of fire and everyone notices her and is very impressed with her. I hope she gets appointed editor of the school paper. She's a natural.

But when she's on the sidelines and someone else is in charge, she can fade into the background. Just then, in spite of her glittery sweater, she seemed to become part of the shadows around her. I already knew she and Wally weren't going to get along, and that she was in for another miserable evening. Her eyes met mine and I could see that how-could-you-do-this-to-me look in them.

After a little bit Daphne took us girls up to her room. It was huge, looking out onto a rolling lawn and a tennis court. The walls were papered with green and pink stripes, and the carpet was a soft green. Daphne had a lot of cute teddy bears and more perfume bottles than I'd ever seen in anyone's room. In the hall I saw Daphne's younger brothers and sisters, but the house was so big that no one was underfoot.

When we went back downstairs, the guys were out on a large veranda in the back, eating snacks. We all joined our dates, except Thelma, who stayed on the opposite side of the patio from Wally.

I kept watching to see how they would get along. But they didn't. Wally was talking to Kent about sports. Wally had been on the Broxton basketball team.

Wally goaded Stanley about not being an athlete, but he couldn't get a rise out of Stanley. "Sports isn't one of my priorities," Stanley said. "I don't have half enough time to spend on my science projects as it is. I'm busy just going to the places that want me to display my invention. Mr. Grayson signed me up to go to a school next Thursday, and now that I've made some improvements in it, NASA wants me to bring it out to their headquarters again so they can check it."

"What is this invention?" Wally asked a little skeptically.

"A vehicle designed to navigate on the rocky surfaces of other planets."

Wally's eyes, behind his magnifying glasses, became unusually large as if he thought Stanley was truly a weirdo.

Lee Ann grabbed the spotlight. "Brian and I are going to Japan next summer," she told Wally. "Our orchestra is going to give a concert in Tokyo."

"I might climb Mount Fuji while we're there," Brian added.

A table had been set up on the veranda, and a maid was busy getting ready to serve. Daphne told everyone where to sit. She placed Thelma and Wally together. I was across from them and I heard Wally ask Thelma if she was a tennis player.

"No," Thelma said. She could have gone on to ask him about his tournament, but she didn't. I wanted to kick her under the table.

"Have you got any acceptances from colleges yet?" was his next question.

"I'm a junior," Thelma answered, which widened the gap between them. Since she didn't express any interest in whether Wally had been accepted, he dismissed her with a superior look and turned to Stanley.

"Where are you going to college, Stoneman?" he asked.

"Don't know yet. Still waiting. MIT, I hope."

"That's pretty far away," Wally said. My heart gave a little twist to think of Stanley being on the opposite side of the United States.

"I'm either going to Stanford, UCLA, or UC Santa Barbara," Daphne said. "I don't know if my grades will get me into Stanford, but my mother went there, which might make a difference."

"I hope I get into Stanford," Wally said. "They have a great tennis team."

"I know someone with a four-point-oh average who got rejected there," Daphne commented.

"Not that I have a four-point-oh, but I've got my fingers crossed," Wally said.

Even though I was a junior, I plunged into the conversation.

"Where should I go to be a pediatrician?" I asked.

"There are lots of good medical schools. Johns Hopkins, for instance," Stanley said.

I tried to get Thelma into the conversation. "Thelma's going to be a journalist. What's the best place for her?"

Thelma knew the answer to that question herself. "I already checked it out," she said. "The good journalism schools are both at places called Columbia. One at Columbia, Missouri, and one at Columbia University in New York."

"You better not go to New York," Daphne made a terrorized face. "People get mugged there."

"If you're going to be in the news business, you have to take a few risks, right, Thelma?" I asked.

"I suppose so." Thelma was still too overwhelmed by these wealthy seniors to relax.

Brian stopped all the college talk when he put a cotton doughnut on the French pastry dessert tray, and Kent picked it up and bit into it.

Then Wally remarked, "My mother applied for an exchange student to live at our house for six weeks. We just heard that we're about to get one from France." He poked his elbow into Stanley's arm. "How do you like that? A French mademoiselle living at our house. I'm brushing up my French."

Thelma gave up any pretense of being friendly with Wally then. I got impatient with her. Thelma probably had a lot more on the ball than any exotic exchange student. She was good at interviewing people, and she knew a lot about a lot of things because she read so much. She could make interesting conversation and be amusing when she was horsing around with Lee Ann and me. She didn't need to pull inside herself and become a small, dark blob as she was doing then. She needed to show Wally how she could sparkle and glow.

"Help get Thelma into the action," I whispered to Stanley. "She's not having a good time."

Stanley cast a startled glance at Thelma. Then he sort of leaned toward her and said to Wally, "Thelma Arkadian here is the star reporter on the Hillview paper."

"Oh? I hope it's better than the boring sheet they call a paper at Broxton," he said. Now that Stanley seemed interested in Thelma, I hoped that Wally might want to find out why and he just might become more friendly.

I gave Stanley a little *O* made with my thumb and forefinger, and moved over to talk to Brian and Lee Ann.

About ten minutes later Wally started yawning and announced he had to get up early to play tennis and he'd better turn in. He didn't even say a special good night to Thelma. Some date!

# 3

STANLEY AND I dropped Thelma off at her house. Stanley insisted on taking her to her door even though she said he didn't need to. I was proud of him for being so polite. I told him so when he returned to the car.

"I can't help feeling sorry for her," he said. "Why does one guy after another ignore her? I was talking to her at the party, and she's really intelligent."

"I guess that's not what guys like Cory and Wally care about," I said. "Anyway, thanks for being considerate. She needed a guy to pay attention to her."

"I hope that's the last of these disastrous parties," Stanley said. "I gave them a try for you, but now I'm fed up with them. I'm ready to go back to just you and me, like before. There's something forced about people being pushed together, like Thelma and Wally Urquhart. Friendships should just occur naturally, like it did with us."

"You're probably right. I guess that's why a lot of parties you hear about at school end up with people getting stoned or smashed. The kids can't stand each other."

"At least, nobody got smashed at this party, only numbed with boredom. It's still early. You want to stop by my house and look through my telescope? I have it fixed on Saturn."

"Well, just for a minute," I agreed. "Tomorrow's a school day."

We stopped at Stanley's house, where no one was home except a couple of servants. I peered through Stanley's telescope and was disappointed that I couldn't see the rings around Saturn. Stanley told me we'd have to take a trip to a nearby planetarium to get a better look through a more powerful telescope. Then he turned the telescope to other parts of the sky. We saw airy nebulae, red, blue, and yellow stars, and a lot of unidentified lights that winked off and on.

When Stanley's mother and dad came home, they said a quick hi to us and wandered off upstairs. Stanley suddenly lost interest in the universe and got romantic. Sometimes I wonder how I was so lucky as to meet Stanley and to have him love me as much as I love him.

But it couldn't last forever. "I think your mother and dad are up there thinking it's time for me to go home," I said, pulling away from Stanley. "We'd better go."

"Not yet," he insisted.

It took all my willpower to stand my ground, and I finally won out.

On the way to school the next morning Thelma said, "I have to apologize for having a totally wrong impression of Stanley Stoneman. I thought he was a stuffy, rich snob, but last night I found out he's a very human guy, not conceited at all, very warm and caring. Maybe the nicest guy I've ever met."

"I've been telling you that all along," I said, glowing inside and knowing that I was the luckiest girl alive.

"It saved the evening for him to be there," Thelma went on. "What a relief to talk to him, after being stuck with that arrogant Wally—Whatsis. Stanley's a person who knows how to look beyond the surface of things and see what's real inside. He was the only one at that party who realized it was a total downer for me."

"I realized it," I reminded her.

"You, maybe. But Lee Ann and Brian, they were so giggly and frivolous and wrapped up in themselves. Daphne—well, she was too busy being Daphne to worry whether all her guests were having a good time, and Kent was too concerned with whether he'd be able to think of something more to say. That Wally, he doesn't have a sensitive bone in his body. If Stanley hadn't been there, I think I would have given up on the whole human race."

Her enthusiasm began to make me uneasy. "What were you and Stanley talking about, anyway?"

"Oh, everything. He's so brilliant. Is there anything he doesn't know? About space and metals and the history of the universe and microbes. Stuff like that. I was never so impressed with anyone's knowledge. See, he let me know how insignificant it is whether some-one has a real date or not. I spent the time after I got home remembering how he made me feel like a worthwhile individual."

Thelma didn't need to rave about Stanley so extrav-agantly. It was my own fault. I'd asked him to cheer her up. Now it looked as if she were attracted to him. Why couldn't that asinine Wally have had the man-ners to get acquainted with Thelma, which was what he'd been invited for? Why couldn't she have a guy of her own, instead of liking mine?

Other girls had made plays for Stanley—like Katie Gneiss, the pushy president of the junior class. She'd asked Stanley to help her with a project for the science fair. She didn't really care about science, but only pretended to get Stanley's attention. What she really wanted was power. Power over as many guys as possible, and as many activities at school.

Then there were Wanda Zetterquist, the gossip columnist for the school paper, who had made a play for Stanley, and Billie Hoyt, the pom-pom girl.

This was different. I could fight off the others, but when my best friend went overboard for the guy I loved, that was a more delicate matter—especially since I was responsible for thrusting them together.

It went from bad to worse. Later in the day Thelma stopped me in the hall. Her eyes flashed and her cheeks glowed. I knew she was cooking up something.

"After hearing Stanley talk about the metal shop, I thought that it was strange there'd never been an article in the Hillview *Howl* about it. I looked through the files and found out it had been totally ignored. I could write a great article about it. It's a mystery to everyone in school what goes on in there. So I asked Mr. Grayson if I could do a story on it and he was very excited. 'Be my guest,' he said. 'It's about time somebody acknowledged our existence.'"

I couldn't share Thelma's enthusiasm. She wouldn't have dreamed of writing about that noisy, unsightly shop with its heaps of metal scraps, the whine of saws, the glare of blowtorches and welding equipment unless there had been a jewel embedded somewhere in that disorder—namely, Stanley Stoneman.

"I suppose you'll do your research in third period," I said acidly. That was when Stanley was in the shop.

Thelma didn't get the drift of that comment. "Cory is not going to get this assignment," she said. "This time I'm taking Rita Carmody, who is dying to get into photography."

Thelma invaded the metal shop the next day,

although she had to get excused from history to cover the story during third period. I had to endure hearing on the way to school the next day how Rita had taken a picture of Stanley working on the metal saw. "He didn't want to be in it," Thelma added, "but Mr. Grayson made him."

"He doesn't like to be conspicuous. Publicity bugs him," I said. "There are plenty of other kids in there who would give anything to get their pictures in the paper."

"That's what Stanley told Mr. Grayson, but I said, 'You have your face mask on anyway. Nobody'll know who you are.' So he posed for us. Mr. Grayson said I should go visit the auto repair class where some of the kids are putting what they learn in metal shop to practical use. Rita and I are going over there this afternoon. Rita had better not screw up these pictures, because we're going to make a major spread out of them. In fact, I think I'll learn photography myself. Become a photojournalist when I start working."

Stanley was also in the auto repair group. Thelma was showing dangerous signs of becoming obsessed with Stanley. But what could I say without seeming possessive and jealous?

The kicker came on Saturday. Every Saturday afternoon I work at the candy stripers. Stanley knows my schedule, but sometimes he forgets.

"Did you know they're having the Concours d'Élégance Saturday afternoon downtown? All these rare antique cars will be shown. We have to go! There are going to be some really ancient Rollses in it and a Bentley and one of the first Studebakers ever made."

"I can't. Remember? I work at the hospital Saturday afternoons."

"Oh, right. You ought to get your schedule changed. You miss out on a lot by working on Saturday."

"I'm kind of new at the candy stripers to be asking to switch days," I said. "When I've been in longer, I can."

I always go to the hospital an hour early on Saturday, because I'm doing a science project. One of the doctors had given me permission to observe in the intensive care nursery where the premature babies are kept. I plan to be a pediatrician some day, and I'm lucky to have a chance to observe firsthand what's going on.

I was worried when I got to intensive care that particular Saturday because I was asked to stay outside. There was a crisis in the nursery concerning the very baby I'd just started observing. She weighed only two and a half pounds and had been fighting to stay alive.

"What's happened?" I asked the nurse at the desk.

"Baby Lindenberg has respiratory distress and she may not make it. Her lungs aren't well-enough developed."

I watched through the window, but all I could see were doctors and nurses crowded around the incubator. I knew exactly what the baby looked like, though, because I'd seen her just a few days before. She had spindly arms and legs and a pinched little red face. She bristled with wires, tubes, and tapes that kept her alive and alerted the doctors and nurses to any danger she was in.

While I was watching and listening to the beepers in the machine hooked to the baby, the tense crowd around the incubator suddenly broke up and some members of the group turned away. The beeping stopped.

A couple of nurses and a doctor came out of the room, taking off their face masks, and I saw that one of the nurses had tears in her eyes and the other looked grim and steely eyed. "If we'd only had that new medicine available here, we could have saved her," she said.

"It hasn't been approved for distribution yet," Dr. Hummel said gently.

I felt my heart lurch as I realized that Baby Lindenberg had just died only a few feet from me. I was all churned up, eavesdropping on the conversation of the doctors, technicians, and nurses as they wandered out of the room. They seemed bitter that they didn't have a new remedy that could have been shot into the baby's lungs to keep them from collapsing.

"It's too late for this particular baby," Dr. Hummel said, "but maybe the medicine will save one of the other five thousand preemies who die every year of respiratory distress." It depressed me that this tiny human being had only had a life span of one painful week, in spite of all the care the nurses and doctors had given it. So I wasn't very receptive when I reached candy stripers headquarters to be greeted by a babbling DeeDee Banfield.

She lost no time in breaking some unwelcome news. "I saw your boyfriend out with another girl," she said. "They were heading into the antique car show just as I passed by it on my way here. She was a thin, dark girl who was talking a mile a minute."

That news was more than I could take, but I managed to act cool. "Oh, yeah," I said. "She's a friend of mine. She's a reporter for the school paper. She's writing a story about old cars."

"Well, which do you want to do, the cash register or the stock today?" DeeDee asked.

"I guess the stock." I couldn't make happy chatter with people when I had this storm of emotions inside. I needed to be alone after knowing that tiny infant had gasped its last breath. I was one of the few people who even knew that that miniature creature had existed. I needed to grieve for her a few minutes before being bombarded by DeeDee's chitchat or having to be pleasant to the customers at the gift counter.

My mood didn't dissolve in the hard work of rearranging and restocking the gift shop shelves. It got worse. The idea of Thelma going to the antique car show with Stanley pounded in my mind. By the time I got home, I was steaming like the inside of a teakettle ready to blow its spout.

Without even thinking what I was going to say, I phoned Thelma. "How did you like the antique car show?" I asked.

"How did you know I went?"

"Rumors get around."

"When I was doing research in the auto repair class, everyone was talking about the Concours d'Élégance," Thelma said, her voice defensive. "So I went and I ran into Stanley and we got to talking. I didn't actually go with him."

"Maybe you just sort of hung around at the entrance until you saw him coming and then you just happened to join him as he went in." A knot of meanness had tied up my insides and made me say things I might normally think but not say. All the sadness, jealousy, and resentment that had been building up inside me that afternoon I dumped on Thelma.

"What would you expect me to do? Tell him I couldn't walk through the show or watch the parade with him because it might make you mad? He knows everything about those old cars and wanted to tell someone. Why not me? It was very interesting."

"It seems to me you find everything Stanley does interesting: the metal shop, the auto repair class, and now the antique car show."

"I thought you were encouraging Stanley and me to be friends. I thought that was the point of going to those parties, so we could get acquainted."

"Maybe. But I didn't want you to start leaning on him and revolving your life around him."

"I'm not! What's the matter with you, Meg? Why are you so uptight?"

"Why don't you get your own boyfriend and leave mine alone?" As soon as that sentence was out of my mouth, I wished I could suck it back in. Luckily I was on the phone and couldn't see the look on Thelma's face. I was glad Thelma couldn't see mine, either. If Stanley and I had done any good by supporting Thelma at those two parties, I'd undone it all now. I was a green-eyed, selfish creep. I knew it, but I couldn't stop it.

"I'll leave you alone, too!" Thelma's voice trembled with rage. She hung up the phone with a loud bang.

I had a date with Stanley that night. We were going to eat dinner at an Italian restaurant called Dino's, a cozy place where the owner knew us. There was a little alcove where we liked to sit, with a candle in a wax-covered bottle on the table and sawdust on the floor. It was our own private place. A place where we'd had great conversations and solved all the riddles of the universe and cured all the diseases of the human body. We imagined what it would be like when Stanley was an astrophysicist and I was a pediatrician, wishing it didn't take so long to get there.

That night as Dino was ushering us to our nook, I still rankled from a totally rotten day, and from my argument with Thelma, especially.

"How was the antique car show?" I asked with a meaningful lift of my right eyebrow.

"Terrific!" He launched into a rhapsody about the machines. "There was this 1913 Buick, which had an oil can stuck in the side of its engine. Every fifty miles, the driver'd have to stop and give the valves a shot of oil. The oldest car I saw was a neat Peerless Racer from 1904. There were cars I never knew existed. Did you ever hear of a Garford car?" Stanley didn't really expect me to answer, and he just went on. "You know what they had on display? Dream cars. Those were far-out cars that automakers would design and build only one of. Another fun thing was sitting in the rumble seat of an old Model T Ford. Was it ever cramped!" Stanley beamed at remembering the old cars.

"Did Thelma sit in that rumble seat with you?" I asked. Stanley got all flustered at the question, or maybe it was the tone of voice in which I asked it.

"As a matter of fact, she did. How did you know she went?"

"It's all over town. People have been coming up to me and saying they saw my boyfriend out with someone else."

"I don't get it. I asked you and you couldn't go. I knew Thelma was interested in cars, so I asked her if she wanted to go."

"Oh, you didn't just run into her as you were going into the show?"

"No. I asked her when she was checking out the auto repair class on Friday."

I could feel my anger rising again. Thelma had lied to me, showing she really did have her eye on Stanley. He would never have asked her on his own. She must have manipulated him into doing it. Still, it made me furious that it's so easy for girls to fool him. Stanley is a fabulously attractive guy, besides being extremely rich. If he pays any attention to a girl, she'll be hot on his trail from then on. So it bums me out when Stanley is taken in by someone like Thelma, who doesn't have a kernel of interest in old cars. She was just faking it to get to be with Stanley for the afternoon, and to be seen with him—probably by all the kids in school.

Dino put our fettucine on the table and I stabbed at mine with all the irritation I felt.

"Hey, what's the big deal, Meg? You're not angry that I went over there with Thelma?" Stanley was wide-eyed with innocence.

"Did it ever occur to you that Thelma has been following you around ever since last Sunday at Daphne's? And you've been so nice to her that she's getting ideas. In fact, she blasted me up one side and down the other this afternoon when I got on her case for hanging around you all week."

"You chewed her out for that? I thought I was supposed to be encouraging her so she could get her self-esteem back after being dumped by those two so-called dates. You're the one who told me to cheer her up, and now you're mad at me for doing it."

"Maybe I said to pay some attention to her so she wouldn't feel totally ignored. But you didn't have to adopt her. After all, she's been one of my best friends for years and years, and you never gave her the time of day before. So now you suddenly start escorting her around your classes and taking her out on a Saturday afternoon, and what's she supposed to think? That maybe you like her now? The trouble with you is, you always fall for the strategies girls like Thelma and Katie Gneiss use to get your attention. You've got to quit being so gullible."

"Yeah, and I was gullible enough when you went out with Kent and told me there was nothing to it, and also when you went out with Dennis Ridge. And then you get on my back for trying to show a little consideration to one of your friends. Don't you trust anybody? If you don't have confidence in me or your friend, all I can say is you're getting too paranoid for me."

Stanley interspersed his angry accusation with gulps of pasta. His plate was empty, and so was mine.

When Dino came in to get our plates and found us arguing, he crooned that we needed something sweet to round off the evening. Stanley only glowered at Dino and said, "We're ready for a check." Then he started in on me again.

"I never wanted to go to either of those parties, and you knew it and kept asking me to go anyway. If you're not satisfied with the way I am, I've had enough."

"I do like the way you are. You know that. Only we can't isolate ourselves from everyone. We need other people."

Stanley glared down at the table, and I knew I'd pushed him too far. He had run away from home when his parents tried to rule his life and were too critical. I knew he could do the same to me.

After Stanley paid the check, he stood up ready to go. He lurched forward as we left the café, tense and rigid as he'd been when I first met him. In those days, he'd been so unapproachable that the kids at school called him "Old Stoneface." When he and I started being partners in the ballroom dancing class where we met, he'd relaxed and become a charming, lovable guy.

I wished I could put all the words I'd just said to him back in my mouth and swallow them.

STANLEY DROVE ME HOME in sullen silence, and he didn't get out to walk me to my front door. He just reached over me to jerk my door open, but the door wouldn't budge. "I can't do it, you'll have to do it yourself," he said.

I finally wrestled the door open and ran up the walk. I couldn't sleep once I went to bed. The dreadful things I'd said to Thelma and Stanley kept going through my head. I opened the window to get some fresh air, but it got too cold. I tried to read, but it made my eyes burn. I might have dozed off just before dawn, but I couldn't sleep long because my eleven-year-old brother, Kevin, made a racket in the hall.

I got up to yell at him to be quiet, but I felt dizzy and unsteady, and my voice came out in a croak. I realized that something was wrong with me—it was hard to swallow. I crawled back into bed.

I never felt worse in my life, and my mom discovered that I had a fever.

"Something was wrong with me yesterday," I told her when she came in to wake me. "I was a real beast. I had fights with both Thelma and Stanley."

"That often happens when you're about to catch something," Mom said after she'd taken my temperature. "You have a high fever, and you'll have to stay in bed all day."

Luckily my mom is a nurse and she knew just what to do for me. It was a relief to have to stay in bed. I wouldn't have known how to face two of my favorite people after alienating them.

Mom gave me some medicine for my sore throat and it made me doze most of the day. I dreamed about going up into space in Stanley's Paddywhack vehicle. I woke up from this fantasy to remember the awful truth—that he was mad at me.

During one of my awake times, Mom told me that Lee Ann had come by to see me but had been sent away because I was contagious. Another time she told me that Stanley had telephoned, but she didn't want to disturb me and told him I was sick.

I came wide-awake then and sat bolt upright in bed. "You should have wakened me. What did he say? Do you think he'll call back?"

"Calm down, honey," Mom said. "You see, these calls and visits only get you excited. You have to rest. That's the only way you'll get well. No, he didn't say anything except 'oh,' when I told him you were sick."

I fretted about what he had wanted. Maybe he'd thought of something else I'd done wrong that he wanted to twit me about. On the other hand, maybe he wanted to apologize for being surly. I began to feel a little better. Surely, he wouldn't have phoned me at all unless he wanted to make up. If he didn't want any more to do with me, he wouldn't have called.

My mom had to go to work on the late-afternoon shift and my dad was busy so my grandpa came in to stay with me.

"Grandpa," I asked. "Did Grandma ever get jealous of you when you were young—I mean, before you were married?"

My grandpa gave a big, satisfied grin. "You betcha!" he exclaimed. He gave me a mischievous wink. "I was quite the catch in those days. It was a feather in your grandma's cap that she snared me, but I didn't come easy."

"Did you and she ever fight in those days?"

"We had some that lasted a few rounds."

"Over other girls?"

Grandpa got a devilish gleam in his eye. "There was the time May Belle York invited me to her family reunion, this big picnic out at the beach. That really outraged your grandma, who thought she'd staked out a claim on me. The fur was flying when Lavinia got at us. I don't know which one of us got the worst of that, May Belle or me. And she got miffed again when the Jensens had a summer visitor from Kansas City and asked me over to entertain her. Tall, willowy girl with raven black hair. The whole town heard about how the Jensens had picked me to squire her around."

"Grandpa, you must have been something."

"I did my share of swashbuckling."

"When you and Grandma fought about these other girls, how did you make up?"

"Well, Meg, you know what a determined lady your grandma is. She was no different when she was young. Wouldn't let anything stand in the way of getting what she wanted—and what she wanted was me. So she'd come around, sweet as pie, with one clever scheme after another to break up me and whatever girl was interested in me at the time."

Grandpa was enjoying himself, telling me about his old girlfriends, and I had just decided that I had the cutest grandpa in the world when my grandma came in, bringing a custard she'd baked for me. She reminded Grandpa that he'd promised to go out with a neighbor, who was waiting for him at their house. Grandpa made his exit.

"What was Milford looking so smug about?" Grandma asked.

"He was just telling me about his old girlfriends before he was married."

Grandma looked wary. "Like who?"

"Some summer visitor that he had to entertain, for instance."

"Dolly Farquhar! A homely priss who hung around here for the whole summer."

"Well, how did you get Grandpa back, if he was the one the Jensens picked to take her out?"

"I didn't try to get him back. I had plenty of fellows wanting to court me that summer. Turner Gambell was sweet on me then. Forrest Chapman hung around constantly, mooning about me. I didn't have time to worry about what Milford was doing."

"Grandma, you must have been pretty terrific. Didn't Grandpa get jealous?"

"Oh, indeed he did! Why do you think he'd hang around someone like Dolly, if not to try to make me jealous? Dolly and he weren't suited at all, and I put a stop to it by telling that nuisance, Forrest Chapman, that Dolly liked him and was always asking about him. Forrest fell for the bait and Grandpa came crawling back to me like a wounded pup. Now, why are you so interested in our long-ago love life?"

"It's just—things don't always go okay between couples, and I wondered if it had always been that way."

"Since the human race began," Grandma assured me. "You and Stanley aren't on the outs?"

I told her about how I'd asked Stanley to be nice to Thelma and how Thelma'd latched onto Stanley.

"Why, you and Thelma have been buddies for years. She wouldn't do that."

"I'm afraid she would. She went to the antique car show with him."

"Didn't you get first choice at going with him?"

"How did you know that, Grandma?"

"I have my sources."

"Grandma!"

"You figure it out. You're not the only person who confides in me, you know."

"What have you been up to, Grandma?"

"You know, Stanley and I are pretty good friends. He was always underfoot when he ran away from home. So who do you suppose he turned to when he was having trouble with his girlfriend?"

"You haven't been talking about me behind my back, and to Stanley, of all people."

"Can you think of anyone who's more of an authority on the subject?"

"Grandma, what did you tell him?"

"I didn't tell him anything. I just listened."

"So what did you hear?"

"I heard that he was unfairly treated. That when you couldn't go, he thought you'd be pleased if he took Thelma. He said you asked him to be nice to her."

"Maybe I did, but I only meant at Daphne's party. I didn't expect her to stick to him like a burr."

"That's your side of it?"

"Part of it. He also brought up the times I'd gone out with Kent and Dennis. He didn't need to drag them in, after we'd already decided they didn't matter."

"That's what happens when you quarrel. You're on the defensive, so you dredge up every grievance you ever had about your opponent."

"I wouldn't exactly call Stanley an opponent."

"Well, good, because he doesn't think you are, either. He wanted to come and see you, but I told him your mother thought you were contagious."

"It wouldn't have hurt. He could have worn a face mask like we do at the hospital."

"You want to see him?"

"Radically. I think I'm getting much better."

"That's the spirit. I hope this is your last fight with Stanley. It causes too much misery for you both."

Stanley must have been waiting at my grandma's house to get the verdict on whether I wanted to see him. It was only a short time before he rushed into my room as if he'd been blasted out of a rocket. I cringed against my pillows. "Don't come too close. You might catch something," I said.

"Your grandmother said it was okay to come over."

"So you've been working on her sympathies again."

Stanley smiled down at me. "She said you might miss me. That it might do you good if I came."

I wanted him to kiss me, but I knew he shouldn't, so I just held out my hand toward his and he grabbed it. That made me feel much better.

"The reason I was such a witch was that I was

coming down with this cold or whatever it is," I explained. "But I guess I shouldn't blame it on that. I should take the blame for being jealous."

"I didn't think you'd care that I took Thelma to the show because it was your idea for me to be nice to her. It made her feel good to go out. Instead of acting moody like she did at the party, she laughed and had fun."

"I was afraid she might get attached to you."

"But she knows I'm attached to you."

"The thing to do is for us to find someone else for her. You could get one of the guys you know interested in her. That shouldn't be hard. After all, she's pretty terrific so it should be easy to find her a boyfriend. Wally Urquhart was a bad choice for her."

"Terrible," Stanley agreed. He shrugged. "I never fixed anyone up. I wouldn't know how to go about it."

"You could, for instance, pick some guy, like in your metal shop, and say, 'You remember that sharp reporter who was in here doing the story on the shop for the school paper? She was asking who you were. I think she might like you.' That might work."

"Good idea, but that might just build up the guy's ego. It wouldn't necessarily get him to ask her out."

"Let's think of a specific event he could ask her to. I know," I said. "We could get two extra tickets to the school play on Friday. They only cost fifty cents. And you could say, 'I happen to have a couple extra tickets to *A Thousand Clowns*. Have you got your tickets yet?' Then if he said no, you could say, 'Be my guest. I'll bet that reporter would like to see it, too. I just happen to have her phone number here.' "

Stanley gave me a crooked smile. "It sounds pretty obvious, and I'm sure to get caught in a lie. Whoever he was, he'd soon find out she hadn't really asked about him. What a whopper!"

"But it's a good kind of a spoof, told to make somebody happy. Just so Thelma won't know we put this guy, whoever he may be, up to it make him promise he won't mention that you gave him the tickets or said she liked him. He's just to make her think he saw her reporting the story in the metal shop and thought she might like to go to the play."

"I can't think of any guy she'd be sure to like, but if you really want me to, I'll see if I can swing it."

"I hope you will, because I get worried about Thelma. She's changed. She used to be full of schemes and fun to be with, but lately, she's been withdrawing from everything except the Hillview *Howl*. Now she's practically obsessed with it."

It made me feel good that we could discuss the problem of Thelma and think up a solution together. Stanley and I were back into our wonderful partnership again.

"I didn't mean any of those things I said to you at Dino's, and you can forget them. I found out I can't get along without you," he said.

"I can't do without you, either," I said. "Some of the things you said at Dino's were okay to say. Like, you said you didn't want to change. You were right.

I'm sorry I made you go to those boring parties. I don't want you to change. I don't even want a single molecule of you to be different."

"There's never going to be any girl for me but you, and we're not going to have any more arguments. It's too painful," he said.

"Grandma says everybody, even if they love each other, argues. But if we do, we have to talk it out and solve it like we just did. Then everything will always be okay."

I gave Stanley fifty cents to buy a ticket for Thelma. He said I didn't need to, that he'd buy both tickets but I felt obligated, because it was my idea. "You only need to pay for the guy," I said.

He looked worried. "I can't think of who the guy is going to be," he said.

"You'll think of someone."

I'm a person who heals fast, and I was able to go back to school after a couple of days in bed. Stanley was all keyed up waiting for news from the colleges he'd applied to. He wanted to go to MIT, but his parents wanted him to go to Stanford. We were studying in the library when he got out the atlas and showed me where MIT was. My heart did a flip-flop when I saw that it was clear across the United States, in Massachusetts, which is about as far away as you can get from California. Realizing that he might go so far away made a big lump come to my throat. He'd be all wrapped up in science, and maybe meet a girl from there who would make him forget about me.

"I ought to hear whether I've been accepted in the next few weeks," he said. "The suspense is terrible."

I was only beginning to think about applying for college when I was a senior, and I knew I could never think of going as far away as Massachusetts. So the combination of me and Stanley seemed headed for doom.

On our way out of the library, Stanley changed the subject so I quit thinking of MIT. "Oh, by the way, I found a guy in metal shop who I thought would go for our scheme to get Thelma out of the doldrums, and I think it's working. Anyway, he looked very impressed when I told him she might like him, and he accepted the tickets."

"He'd better not ask someone else," I said. "Is he cute?"

"His name is Jimmy Pollard. He's really good at shaping metal. Instead of making heavy machine parts like I do, he goes at it from a more artistic angle. He made a metal wall plaque with flowers and butterflies for his mother. It was very intricate, and took a lot of skill. That's not my kind of metal working at all, but still, he designed this project himself, and it's fascinating to see how he gets different shades of gold out of heating up the metal with the blowtorch."

"But what does he look like?" I asked.

"Brown hair, brown eyes, you know the type."

"Oh, Stanley, you can be more detailed than that."

Stanley shrugged. "He's a good-natured guy, friendly, always smiling, like that."

"So you gave him Thelma's phone number?"

"Yeah, he has it."

"You and I should go to see *A Thousand Clowns* so we can see how they get along."

"I guess we could go. Actually, I was planning to work on a video. I'm putting together a lot of tapes of space exploration. It is going to be so neat. When the Paddywhack is perfected, it's going to have a built-in video camera."

"You could do that and go to the play, too. The play isn't more than two hours long, and you can't work all the time."

"Well, okay, if you'll work with me on the video beforehand."

Actually, I like to work with Stanley on his projects, because he gets so excited about them. They're really his way of having fun, and Stanley is at his most vibrant when he's absorbed in his inventions.

So we went to the play. "We don't want to interfere with Thelma's date," I told him. "So we'll sit as far away from Thelma and Jimmy as possible."

It turned out that we had a hard time finding a parking place, and so we got in slightly after the play had begun. We had to sit on the side in the back row. When the lights went on at the end of the play, I stood up and looked around the audience, curious to see what Jimmy Pollard was like. There was such a mob that it was hard to spot anyone.

"Come on," Stanley urged. "Let's beat the crowd to the parking lot."

As I was going out one door, I saw Thelma coming out the other. She looked as if she was alone. Then I saw a boy trailing behind her. But it couldn't be Jimmy Pollard. He was more than half a head shorter than she was, and he looked as if he might be her younger brother. He was a pink-cheeked, immature-looking kid who was surely a freshman. I gave Stanley an alarmed look and nudged him in the side.

"That little kid behind Thelma isn't her date, is it?" I demanded.

"Sure. That's Jimmy. Let's go over and find out how it went."

I didn't think that was a good idea, but Stanley was already elbowing his way through the crowd toward them.

"Hi, Jimmy. How'd you like the play?" Stanley greeted him.

Thelma turned around at his voice and I could see an explosion of understanding on her face. She looked at me and her expression changed to one of anger.

"It was great," Jimmy said. "A barrel of laughs."

Though I could tell Thelma had figured out Stanley and I were responsible for her blind date, I tried to act innocent. "I didn't know you were coming to the play," I said.

"You didn't?" She said it in a tone that told me she had it all figured out.

"We better get to our car before the traffic jam starts," Stanley said, and the crowd separated Thelma and Jimmy from Stanley and me.

On the way home, the look on Thelma's face haunted me. She had definitely guessed, and our long friendship was probably doomed. I was so irritated at Stanley I finally burst out with it.

"Did you actually think that Jimmy Pollard was a suitable date for Thelma?" I asked. "What is he, anyway, a freshman? And he was a good five inches shorter than Thelma. She looked bummed out."

Stanley glanced around with his bewildered look. "Jimmy's a nice kid," he said. "And you can't criticize a person just because he's short. I don't know how old he is. Anybody can take metal shop."

"But you should have picked somebody older and more mature," I continued. I didn't want to get in another quarrel with Stanley, yet I had to let him know that Jimmy Pollard was a mistake.

"But I thought the idea was to get somebody who would be terrifically impressed with Thelma, to build up her ego, and Jimmy was all agog to think he was going to take this important reporter out. I thought I'd done something good."

"Also, it wasn't a good idea to rush over and speak to Jimmy," I scolded. "I'm afraid that made Thelma wise to the fact that we had set up the date."

"Do you realize," Stanley said, "that ever since that party at Lee Ann's I've been in hot water with you—all because of your friends? We were better off just by ourselves."

"We can't cut ourselves off from the human race," I

reminded him. "And I hope this episode hasn't alienated Thelma. We'll have to make it up to her somehow. Maybe you could find someone a little more sophisticated and we could be more subtle about it this time."

"Not again!" Stanley exclaimed. "Spare me!"

## 5

I TELEPHONED THELMA to try to smooth things over. I wished I hadn't, when I heard what she had to say.

"So you and Stanley were behind that joke with that freshman! How do you think I felt when he came to get me and his mother was driving? If it was your intention to humiliate me, you certainly succeeded. When I walked into the auditorium with this total infant, who did I see first? Cory Watkins just one row behind me with some terrific-looking girl. It wasn't only a cruel joke on me, but on that kid, Jimmy, too. He felt out of it, and he confessed to me on the way home that he'd gotten the tickets and my phone number from Stanley. He said you told him I'd noticed him while I was doing the story on the metal shop. How can you have no respect for me at all? Don't wait for me to walk with you on Monday or ever again."

She slammed down the phone before I could even try to explain. Or was there an explanation for what we'd done? Actually, for what Stanley had done, because I hadn't even known Jimmy Pollard.

I was glad when Lee Ann dropped by my house later that day. I could always depend on her to be cheerful. Or so I thought. On that particular day, she seemed distracted, as if she had something on her mind.

So finally I came right out and asked her. She was sort of staring into space. I waggled my hand in front of her eyes. "What did I just say?" I asked.

Lee Ann was startled to attention. "Oh, sorry, was I daydreaming?"

"You tell me," I said. "You look like you're worried about something."

"Actually, I am. I didn't want to bother you with it, but now that you ask . . ." She hesitated.

"Okay, let's have it."

"It's Brian. He got an F on a physics quiz this week."

"That's not the end of the world. Everybody messes up on a quiz once in a while. There's still a lot of time in the quarter. He can do better next week."

"He says he can't. It's way over his head. He doesn't get it."

"He should go in for extra help from the teacher."

"He says the teacher is a bear. He's scared the teacher will think he's a dork if he admits he hasn't a clue."

"Then there's nothing you can do about it. It's his problem. Let him worry about it."

"But it *is* my problem. All year we've been just living for our summer trip overseas with the orchestra. But one of the requirements for going is that you have to have a B average. So if Brian flunks physics, he'll be disqualified. I don't want to go if he doesn't, so that would be the end of our dream. We've been reading stacks of books about Japan and all we talk about is what we're going to do there. So can't you see that Brian's F destroys *everything?* There's nothing to look forward to if he's knocked out of the trip. Our lives aren't worth living."

"Now, Lee Ann! It's not really that bad. Even if you and Brian went to Japan, it would be over in a few weeks, and you'd have to come back and find something else to be interested in. Look on the bright side. Brian might suddenly start listening in class and get the picture."

Lee Ann's head shook slowly back and forth. "If you only knew how low Brian's spirits are. He's already imagining this freshman who is the only other oboe player, and a terrible one at that, taking his place and ruining the concert. It isn't fair. Maybe Brian can't understand physics, but he doesn't need it to be a good oboe player."

I had to agree, and then I had an inspiration. "I

happen to have an in with the top physics student in school!" I exclaimed.

"Stanley, of course," Lee Ann said mournfully. "It's hardly fair for one person to be that good and for another not to have a clue what's going on."

"That's how the world operates," I said. "All people have different skills and talents. If you gave Stanley an oboe, he'd be an idiot. But what I was thinking was, maybe Stanley could work with Brian before his next test. Explain things so he'd get it. Stanley is very good at explaining. Remember when the *Voyager* was going around Neptune? We watched it all night, and he explained to me how the *Voyager* worked. I understood it very clearly. It would be easy for him to explain physics to Brian. Stanley could make it so clear to him he'd sail right through the rest of the quarter."

"And get a B? I can't imagine it."

"Why not try? It can't hurt. Brian has no place to go but up."

"Will you set it up with Stanley? Brian would never have the nerve to ask him."

"Sure. No problem."

But after Lee Ann left, I wondered if I'd gone out on a limb again. Was I pushing Stanley into something he wouldn't want to be involved in? Was I using him? Would this cause more trouble between us?

So I introduced the subject to Stanley very cautiously. "You remember Brian Hotchkiss, the oboe player?"

"Sure. Nice guy."

"And the trip he was planning to take with the orchestra to Tokyo?"

"Yeah. Sounds like a blast."

"But it turns out that he might not get to go, after all." I explained Brian's dilemma to Stanley.

"I can't believe anybody can have trouble with physics. The most logical thing in the world."

"But not everybody's mind works like yours. Brian got a flat-out F."

Stanley gave an incredulous whistle.

"It would be great if somebody could explain it to him, somebody who was really good at it and good at explaining."

"I'm good at it, but I don't really know him that well."

"If you worked with him, you'd get to know him better."

"But what if I couldn't get through to him and he blamed me for wasting his time?" His eyes narrowed and he said, "Like I fouled up with Thelma Arkadian."

I felt guilty about pushing him again. I said, "Oh, well, it's up to you."

His face creased with a superserious frown. "I don't know why I shouldn't. It would be a piece of cake for me. But I'd hate to go up to him and say, 'Hey, Hotchkiss. I hear you're flunking physics. Need any help?' "

"Leave it to me," I said. "I can set up a study

session with Lee Ann. She's desperate for him to qualify for the trip."

"I still feel bad about getting the wrong kind of date for Thelma," Stanley said. "I've been talking to this much bigger guy, Ross Foster, and if you thought it was okay, I could give him her phone number and then I could get it off my mind."

I knew who Ross Foster was, and he was a good-looking guy Thelma would probably be proud to go out with. I didn't know much about him, but he was some kind of a popular jock.

I felt a surge of special love for Stanley. He was probably the most thoughtful guy in the whole world.

"Sure," I said. "Why not? This may be our week to solve everybody's problems."

Lee Ann was delighted that Brian would get help with physics. But just before he started the project, Stanley had second thoughts. "What if I can't get through to him? After all, I'm not a teacher."

"But you make it all clear to me. Remember how you explained all about force and velocity and energy to me when you showed me the Paddywhack? You made it so simple."

Stanley looked optimistic. "You learn fast," he said, "but maybe Brian doesn't."

"You have to try. I've already told them you would, and it's his only chance."

"This all started when you asked me to go to Lee Ann's party that night. I got involved with all those friends of yours and their problems. First Thelma and her trouble getting a boyfriend. Now Brian and his denseness about physics. What next?"

"But you are going to do it, aren't you?"

"Sure. Brian is a nice guy, and I like him, so I will. And by the way, I gave Ross Foster Thelma's phone number. But this is the last time. Promise you won't ask me to solve any more of your friends' dilemmas."

After that, things turned out okay for me. Stanley started coaching Brian, and Lee Ann reported that Brian was seeing the light. Then, unexpectedly, Thelma started walking to school with me again. One morning she was walking slowly just ahead of me, and she stopped to wait for me, and then she started talking just as if no disagreement had ever happened between us.

"You'll never guess what happened!" she began.

"What?" I asked, trying to act as if I weren't surprised by her reappearance.

"Out of the blue, I got a phone call last night from the most unlikely person."

"Who?"

"You're not going to believe this—Ross Foster. You know who he is, I hope. A tackle on the football team."

My heart was jumping in my chest, and I was afraid my face might give away what I knew about this phone call. Should Stanley have done it? Should I have goaded him into it? "What did he want?" My voice sounded hollow.

"He asked me to a party. It's going to be over at

Greg Tinsley's on Friday night. Gosh, Meg, I had to talk to you. I didn't know what to *say*. I know who Ross Foster is, but that's it. It's not often that a person gets to go out with football players, so like a dope, I said, 'Well, I guess I have Friday night free.' And he says, 'Pick you up at eight o'clock. Tell me how to get to your house.' I'm just on pins and needles, Meg, thinking I shouldn't accept a date with such a stranger, but it was too much of a temptation."

"Yeah, I can imagine." I wanted to swallow my tongue.

Thelma kept making me feel worse by consulting me on whether she should wear this or that, and whether I thought the people at Greg's party would think she was cool or not.

Meanwhile, Stanley's tutoring of Brian seemed to be working.

"Brian said he wants to take you and me out for hamburgers on Friday night to celebrate his mastery of the basic laws of physics," Stanley said. "One way I got to him was by explaining the physical laws of sound, like what's happening when he blows on his oboe. He's so excited about it that I think we ought to go out with him."

"Sure," I said. "That would be fun."

And it was. Lee Ann and Brian were in their usual bubbly moods, and they were chattering hopefully again about their trip to Tokyo. Stanley felt free to discuss some of his scientific ideas, since he had clued Brian in on the subject.

"Did you hear Thelma was going to this party over at one of the jocks' house?" Lee Ann said.

"Yes," I said guardedly. "I wonder how it's going."

"I'd be scared to go to a party at some stranger's," Lee Ann said. "Especially with all those jocks. They sometimes get wild."

"They can't have those ragers anymore," Brian said. "Did you hear that there's now a juvenile alcohol party law in town? If anybody has a party with more than ten people and anybody under twenty-one is drinking anything or anybody has drugs there, they'll arrest the host, and all the guests will get in trouble."

"My dad said it's about time they cracked down on kids who hold those keggers when their parents are gone," I said.

Then Brian and Stanley started discussing physics, and Lee Ann told me a funny story about her dog.

The next morning at breakfast my dad looked up from the paper and remarked that the first arrest had been made under the new party law. "A Greg Tinsley. Parents were out of town for the weekend. A couple of dozen teenagers raising Cain in the house, and the neighbors complained."

I felt the hair on my arms prickling. Thelma was one of the couple of dozen kids, and I wondered what trouble she was in. Also, I wondered if she had figured out that Stanley had engineered her date. I felt a twinge of anger toward Stanley. While trying to make up for picking one unsuitable date for her, he'd picked a second, even worse one. Did she know Stanley was responsible? My curiosity couldn't be contained. I telephoned her.

"What's happening?" I asked.

"Disaster," she said. "Don't you read the papers?"

I played dumb.

"It's all over the front page," she said. "Greg Tinsley's party was raided. What a mess! Everybody was out of hand. I started to leave at one point, and I wish I had. Ross Foster is the stupidest dweeb imaginable. And don't think I didn't find out how he happened to call me. He told me. 'It's lucky Stoneman heard me beefing about needing a date for this bash, or I never would have met you,' he said, and once I saw the kind of action he was letting me in for, I wished he never had. Where do you and Stanley get off, horning in on my life time after time?"

"I didn't have anything to do with that," I assured her. "It was strictly Stanley's idea. He keeps hoping he can connect you up with somebody you'll like."

"Who asked anyone to find me a boyfriend? Who needs one?" Thelma exclaimed. "All they cause is trouble. All of us would have been better off if none of us had ever started dating. You're always busy with your egghead genius, and Lee Ann isn't the same since she met Brian Hotchkiss. Neither of you is fun to be with anymore. And as for the two losers Stanley picked for me, I prefer my own company."

I didn't know what to say, but I didn't have to say anything, because Thelma kept running on. "Do you know what you got me into? Everybody caught at that party is in the town's juvenile detention program. Any of us caught at a similar party in the next two years will have a permanent police record."

Thelma, the good student and model citizen, was the last person I could imagine having a police record.

"Besides, we all have to do eight hours of community service: sweeping sidewalks, picking up trash, or painting fire hydrants and light poles, stuff like that. You guys have practically wrecked my life. My parents are coming down hard on me and I won't get to do anything for months. They don't trust me anymore. It will be all around school that I was mixed up in that orgy. Do you think Miss Wagstaff will want someone on detention to edit the school paper next year? You and your great Stanley Stoneman have done the last damage you'll do to me, because I no longer consider you my friends. And this time it's permanent."

The bitterness in her voice gave me a feeling like I'd just eaten a stone and it was weighing down my stomach. It's hard to lose a friend who's been as close as Thelma.

I couldn't help getting on Stanley's case about picking such a gross guy to take Thelma on a date.

"I hardly knew him." Stanley defended himself, his eyes round and innocent. "You said the other guy, Jimmy, was too young and small for her. So I see this guy with muscles, and I could see he's a guy who's been around, and I thought, this is who I should have fixed Thelma up with. Then when I heard he was

70

looking for a date, I thought it was destiny or something like that."

"Destiny! She figures her life is ruined and she's permanently mad at me. When you pull a trick like this, I wonder where your brains are."

Stanley is not a person you can push too far, and apparently I was doing it.

"This whole month you've been on my case," he said. "Forcing me to go to those parties I didn't want to go to, then getting me stuck with your unhappy friend and complaining when I try to repair her social problems. You know where I've been for the last hour? Trying to pound some physics into your other girlfriend's boyfriend. You're never satisfied. Sometimes I wonder how I ever got mixed up with you in the first place. You keep pushing your incompetent, depressing friends on me, expecting me to put their lives together. I've had enough, and since you keep wanting to change me, I guess you've had enough of me, too. We better forget about each other."

I was totally speechless. Forget about Stanley! My world had revolved around him for most of the school year. A lump formed in my throat and tears fought at my eyelids. But I held them back. I've never been a crier.

"I may still try to get Brian through that course, since I promised, but after that, I'm concentrating on my inventions and getting ready for the science fair, and goodbye to you and your friends."

I turned and walked away. I didn't want him to see

me losing control. I wish I could have been cool and argued him out of it, but he had that stern and immovable look that said he was serious about getting me out of his life.

I remembered Thelma's question: "Who needs a boyfriend?" The answer was me. I needed Stanley. Now that I'd had him for all that time, I knew I'd be a wreck without him. Stanley had spread the universe and all its history before me. How could I shrink back into my old small world?

# 6

On Wednesday there was lots of news at the hospital. Daphne was all aglow, her porcelain complexion illuminated by a tinge of excitement. Her golden hair jiggled from a pink band in a wavy ponytail.

"The French exchange student has arrived at the Urquharts!" she exclaimed. "Wally was expecting a girl, but it turned out to be a guy. Dark hair and eyes, tall, a tennis player, and the minute those dark eyes made contact with mine, we knew we were going to be a twosome. So I've been invited to the Urquharts' beach cabin for the weekend. Can you imagine anything more fantastic? I don't know how I can wait for two whole days. I won't be coming in for my Saturday duty, of course, I'll make it up some other day."

"I thought you and Kent were going out Saturday night."

"Oh, well, Kent will understand. Étienne will only be here for a few weeks—it's one of those short student exchanges—and I can see Kent any time."

I had flower cart duty with one of the other girls, and as I delivered the flowers and gifts I remembered how Daphne had become infatuated with Kent on this same run.

I had predicted at the time that she'd lose interest in Kent before long and now it had happened. Kent wasn't going to understand at all. He took Daphne seriously, and I was afraid he'd be deeply hurt when she broke her date with him. It was likely that Daphne and Kent would never get together again. Daphne just took on guys as temporary amusements, flitting from one to another.

After my work was over, I went up to the preemie nursery. There was no use rushing home, since I wouldn't be getting together with Stanley. He'd be holed up with his science magazines, congratulating himself for breaking up with me. How could he have said those things to me only a few days after we'd made up from our last fight?

In the intensive care nursery, Dr. Hummel showed me a brand-new preemie. It weighed two pounds, and he said it had a seventy percent chance of living. One of the older babies had gained enough weight so that it would go home in three days.

I admire Dr. Hummel and the nurses. They have to be on their toes all the time because so much can happen to their teeny patients.

I was leaving for the day, passing by the gastrointestinal section, when I saw a familiar face in the hall.

"Mrs. Arkadian?" I said, recognizing Thelma's mother. "What are you doing here? Visiting a friend?"

"It's Mr. Arkadian," she said. "He's had problems with an ulcer for the last few years, but today he had so much pain that the doctor said he'd have to come in for tests." Mrs. Arkadian's face was drawn and she looked scared.

"Can I help?" I asked. "I just finished my shift, but if there's anything you need, just ask."

Mrs. Arkadian's eyes were red and puffy as if she'd been crying, and I knew Thelma's dad must be in some danger.

"Maybe you could go over to keep Thelma company," her mother said. "She's been so depressed recently, and this is so upsetting that I didn't want her to be here while the tests were in progress. She's trying to hold down the fort at home, and maybe it would ease the tension if you went over and kept her company."

Thelma obviously hadn't told her mom we had fought. Right then it didn't seem to matter. This was one of those times when disagreements had to be shoved into the background.

"Sure. I've got the whole evening free. I'll go over and see if I can help."

Mrs. Arkadian gave me a hug and I could feel the tears on her cheeks. I felt almost like one of the family, since I'd spent so much time at their house through the years. I hated for Mr. Arkadian to be sick. He'd always been so good to me. He was assistant manager of the Stars and Stripes Amusement Park, where he arranged many freebies for us.

After I had changed out of my pinafore, I hurried out of the antiseptic-scented lobby of the hospital and into the fresh spring air, planning what I'd say to Thelma. She probably wouldn't want to see me, but I had to make her be my friend again.

Thelma's house was on my way home from the hospital. When I rang the doorbell and Thelma answered, I could see that she was going through an ordeal. Her family crisis seemed to have driven our disagreement out of her mind, so she invited me in right away. As if we'd never quarrelled, I put my arms around Thelma. "I saw your mom at the hospital," I said. "She told me what had happened, so I came over to keep you company."

"I suppose you realize it's all my fault—what's happened to my dad."

"What do you mean? He's had that ulcer for a long time. I've always heard how we have to behave because of your dad's ulcer. Remember that time somebody got hurt on the roller coaster at the amusement park and you told me it made your dad's ulcer act up. So how could you be to blame for something that's been bothering him for so long?"

"It's that stupid party, and my getting caught at it. I can't remember anything that hit him so hard. I've always been the goody-goody honor student and suddenly I'm caught at a wild party. It sort of made him explode inside. Don't you see? I'm responsible."

"Thelma Arkadian! That's ridiculous. You cause your parents a lot less trouble than most kids. You keep your grades up, you don't stay out fooling around at night—"

I was going to list some more of Thelma's good points, but she cut me off. "It's only because I never had a chance to stay out at night and get into trouble. The first time I did, see what happened. My dad can't take it. He has a stressful life running the amusement park. There are always people quitting and he has to hire new ones. Sometimes there are arguments between people who run the food concessions and he has to settle them, and then there are rowdies coming into the park who he has to keep in line. When he comes home from all that, he doesn't need to hear that his daughter's been involved in a raid where kids were drinking and doping."

"You didn't know it was that kind of a party you were going to."

"Because I'm too much of a dork to have been asked to any parties before. Face it, Meg, I'm a loser. I don't look that good, I probably won't get to be editor of the school paper, and I hate my name. Why couldn't they have named me Alison or Kimberly or Stephanie, or something like that? Thelma! To hear it is to hate it! If I wasn't in the world, no one would even notice."

"I'm taking you out for a burger. I won't let you get any deeper into that hole you're digging for yourself."

"But my mom told me to stay here to answer the phone in case anything happens to my dad and I have to phone relatives."

"Well, then, let's put on some music and try to cheer up. Remember, I work at the hospital and I know the doctors and nurses are just great. They're going to pull your dad out of this and get him in shape so that he'll feel better than ever. I've seen it happen a lot. So get happy. You can't do anything about it, and your dad won't appreciate having you come in looking down like you do now. You'll have to go in and visit him with your special glow and tell him about good things happening. Like about some of your stories. I know you're going to be editor next year, because you've had the most original stories in the paper, and you've had more than anyone else. You're just the logical choice."

"You're just saying that. But it would really perk him up if I was made editor. If it wasn't for my dad, though, Meg, I would have been kind of glad I was caught at that party, because a reporter has to have lots of experiences. I'm going over with a bunch of the kids this weekend to do maintenance work at one of the grade schools. That's part of my eight hours of community service."

"Why don't you write a piece for the school paper about it? That would be interesting for everyone. You could describe what happens when you get caught at a rager, and what it's like to be in the juvenile detention program."

"Meg, that's a great idea. Instead of being embarrassed about going out with that work gang, I can use it. Make people think I just went to that dumb party to get material for an article. Miss Wagstaff might admire my initiative and it might be a plus instead of a minus as far as getting to be editor is concerned."

Thelma got so excited about doing an article on the party that the color came back to her cheeks and her black eyes came alive. We started having our usual fun, and I phoned my house to say I was staying at Thelma's for dinner, heating up something in the microwave.

"How come you're not with Stanley today?" Thelma asked.

"Stanley and I had an argument," I told her. I had momentarily forgotten about losing him, but now that the subject came up, I became the gloomy one.

"What about?"

"It's been kind of building up for the past month," I said. "But actually, it was Ross Foster who caused the total blowup." I wished I hadn't said that when I saw Thelma's reaction.

"Then it's my fault again," Thelma said. "If you hadn't had to take me to Daphne's party with you or if Stanley hadn't been worried about finding those blind dates for me, everything would be okay between you. I cause trouble for everybody. Why do you put up with me?"

"Because you're my good friend. Because I care about you," I said. But I knew it was true: Stanley and I wouldn't have been quarrelling so much if it wasn't for Thelma.

"One thing's for sure," Thelma said. "I'm through with guys. All the ones I've met are drips. I'm just going to concentrate on the paper from now on. I'm going to be the greatest reporter the school has ever had. I can hardly wait to do that story on the party."

Thelma had a sudden thought and that defeated look crossed her face again. "Only there's still what I did to my dad," she said. "I can never erase that. I wish my mom would come home and let me know what's going on."

Eventually I had to go home. I worried about Thelma on the way. She was too intense and insecure. It was so easy for her to get on a disaster course. I quit worrying when I got inside my house though. I could smell the wonderful aroma of orange sponge cake baking. "We'll save some of this for Stanley," Mom said. "It's his favorite."

"He won't be around tonight," I said. I didn't want to mention our latest argument. It would make my mom quiz me about Stanley, and it was too painful to talk about.

I squeezed an orange for the frosting and went to

my room, telling her I'd be back to help frost the cake later.

Back in my room, I dumped the contents of my purse on the bed. There was a bulletin from the candy stripers that I hadn't had a chance to read. Now I smoothed it out. Annual Benefit Ball—Hillview Hospital Auxiliary, it said.

It was to be held at the country club. It would be a dinner dance and was going to cost fifty dollars per person. The candy stripers were supposed to sell tickets to it. If Stanley and I hadn't quarrelled, I could have sold him tickets and he and I would have gone. Maybe even his mother and dad would have bought tickets from me. As it was, I couldn't think of anyone who'd want to buy tickets. It wasn't the sort of party my parents or neighbors would go to. Kids at school couldn't afford it. I hoped the other candy stripers would sell enough to make up for me. I tossed the bulletin away. I wouldn't be going.

Daphne telephoned me a bit later. "Have you sold any tickets to the benefit ball?" she asked.

"I haven't had time, and I doubt if I can sell any, anyway."

"How about you and Stanley doubling with me and Étienne?" she asked. "We could get up a whole table. Wally is taking Jennifer Ridley. Étienne bought two for me and him. I also sold four to Sonny who's asked Barbara Gilliland. The other tickets are for his brother, Roger, who will be home from college for that weekend. He doesn't have a date yet, but we're working on it. So how about you and Stanley joining our party?"

I was reluctant to tell Daphne about our breakup, but she'd find out anyway. "Stanley and I had a disagreement," I said, trying to sound offhand. "So we won't be going."

"Oh, haven't you sold tickets to the Stonemans? Could I do it? Would you mind? The one who sells the most tickets gets a prize."

"You're welcome to sell tickets to them."

"Hey, Meg, that gives me another idea. If you aren't going with Stanley, how about being Roger's date for the evening? He already has the tickets, and since he's been away at college, he's lost touch with a lot of the girls here. Perfect! You and he will get along great! You'll do it, won't you? We'll have a blast! I'll even let you dance with Étienne, if you'll promise not to flirt with him."

I was astonished at how matter-of-factly Daphne took the news of my breaking up with Stanley. But then I remembered that Daphne changed boyfriends as readily as she changed outfits. It was no big deal to her.

"You probably don't want to go because you think Roger will be like Sonny," she said after a pause had gone by without my answering. "But he's not. He's tall, good-looking, polite, and, of course, being a college man—a sophomore at UCLA, to be exact—he's really cool. I think you might be his type, too. You will, won't you? And then one of our problems will be solved."

Daphne's enthusiasm was catching. I was eager to go. I didn't need to be loyal to Stanley anymore, since the breakup was his idea, not mine.

"Let me think about it a little," I said.

"What's there to think about? It's a made-to-order situation, and it'll be such fun if we can go together. Don't mind that Sonny will be along. His brother will keep him in line, and you'll like Barbara Gilliland. She's a neat person, kind of a cut-up. So, it's all set, isn't it?"

If I hadn't liked Daphne so much, I wouldn't have taken a chance on accepting a blind date with a college guy, but Daphne seemed so positive about it, what else could I do? In fact, I became very excited about the dance, wishing it would hurry and arrive.

Lee Ann dropped by the next day after school. "Stanley certainly dropped a firecracker under Brian," she said. "Not only does he understand his homework in physics now, but he's interested in it. Stanley's been teaching him all about how sound works, and he's letting Brian come out to his lab to see some of his inventions."

"So Stanley is still working with him?"

"Sure. Wasn't that what he said he'd do?" Lee Ann looked curiously at me. I hadn't told her Stanley and I had broken up. And I didn't then, either. I was suddenly resentful that Brian was taking my place as Stanley's companion in his lab. I doubted that Brian would understand and appreciate Stanley's feverish interest in his inventions the way I did.

"The things Brian has to worry about now are the experiments in class, where he can't ask Stanley questions, and his workbook, which is going to count a third of his grade. So he's not out of the woods, and we're going to be in suspense until the end of the quarter."

Changing the subject, she asked, "Did you talk to Thelma today?"

"I did," I said. "Her dad has to have an operation because the tests yesterday showed that he might have something worse than an ulcer. She's afraid if he's sick a long time he'll lose his job. And do you know, she still blames his illness on her escapade with Ross Foster. But she did get some good out of it. Miss Wagstaff welcomed the idea of her writing an article on the consequences of going to a wild party."

"She's such a workaholic. I'm afraid she's burning herself out. It's a matter of life and death to her to get on the A honor roll. And she figures she has to do twice as much work as anyone else so she can be editor of the *Howl* next year."

"I know," I said. "She's way too intense."

But my own affairs kept me from worrying about Thelma all the time.

"It's all set for you and Roger," Daphne informed me on Saturday at the hospital. Brenda is miffed that I didn't ask her to be Roger's date. So I told her that you and Stanley weren't going together anymore and that I had sold four tickets to the Stonemans. I encouraged her to get Stanley to take her."

That hurt. I missed Stanley unbearably, and suddenly I felt like telling Daphne to cancel my date with Roger. I didn't want to go to that ball if there was a chance of seeing Stanley with someone else.

DeeDee Banfield came down the hall just then and joined us with news that gave me a further jolt. "Guess who I'm going to the benefit ball with?" she asked happily. "Stanley Stoneman. I didn't know you and he had broken up, Meg. But anyway, Mrs. Stoneman called my mother and said she had these tickets and asked me to go with them."

# 7

THE NEXT TIME I ran into Kent Whitehead at school, I said, "You're walking great now."

"Yeah," he agreed tonelessly.

"It must feel good to be free of that cast."

"I guess so."

"Kent! What's the matter? You act like you've lost your last friend."

"Maybe I have."

"Explain," I demanded. "Tell me why you're down."

"You ought to know."

"Is it something I've done?"

"It's—well, Daphne. She doesn't call me up anymore. When I call her, she's busy."

This was what I'd been afraid of when Daphne made a play for Kent. That she'd get tired of him soon and hurt him by dropping him.

"She's dumped me." Kent gave me an aggrieved look.

"I wouldn't call it dumped, exactly," I said. "The thing is, there's this French exchange student staying next door to her and his host family asked her to help entertain him, so she's just busy. You'll probably see her again after he goes back to France."

"It's not that. She never really like me that much. She just wanted to go out with a guy from Hillview. Now she's done it."

"Don't be so negative, Kent. There are other fish in the sea."

"Not like her."

"Follow her example, Kent. Take someone else out."

"How would she know? I never see her. She said when my leg was healed, she was going to have me over to play tennis. Now she never will."

"Of course she will. She hasn't forgotten you. She's just busy with this foreign student for a while. He won't be here forever."

"It was bad enough missing out on basketball season. Now this."

I couldn't cheer Kent out of his gloomy mood. I

thought about that party we'd had at the beginning of the quarter. None of the pairs who'd attended were still together except Brian and Lee Ann. And they were worried that they might not get to spend the summer together. I told Kent about that, and about Thelma's dad, just to let him know he wasn't the only person with troubles.

"I'm having as bad a time as you," I said. "But I refuse to go around feeling sorry for myself."

"What's bad that's happened to you?"

I told him about quarrelling with Stanley.

"You and Stoneman were a famous twosome," he said, sympathizing. "That's terrible."

"I guess we were together too much and I started getting on his nerves," I said.

"I thought he'd stick to you forever. He was wacko over you."

"Oh, quit it, Kent. Let's drop the subject." I couldn't talk about Stanley any longer. I missed him too much.

After that talk, Kent started hanging around me, appearing at my locker and at various other places where he thought he might run into me. He wasn't coming on to me or anything, he just seemed to want to find out if I was okay, and to talk to someone. Finally he asked me if I wanted to go to a movie with him on Saturday night, but that was the date of the benefit ball. So I had to deal another blow to his ego.

I wasn't in the mood for that ball. It scared me a little to go out with a college man, and especially one who was the brother of the obnoxious Sonny Whitlow. Worse yet, Stanley would be there with DeeDee. I wondered if I could face that. Still, if someone has paid fifty dollars for a ticket to take you somewhere, you're pretty much obligated to go.

Roger Whitlow was a great-looking guy. The minute I saw his long lean, lively, and amiable face at the door, I knew why Sonny is like he is. He's completely overshadowed by his attractive older brother. Roger had an easygoing manner that drew me out immediately. He brought me a yellow-throated white orchid. I'd never had anything like it. He kept saying things that made me feel he was the luckiest guy in town for getting to take me to the ball.

"Nobody told me I'd be going out with a Sally Field look-alike," he said.

"People have said that before," I told him. He was so easy to talk to that I was able to ask him flat out why he would go on a blind date with a high school junior instead of bringing one of his college friends.

"Since this was a candy stripers' affair, and Daphne had sold me the tickets, I wanted to join her party with one of her friends. A lucky decision for me." Roger gave me a wink that might have turned my heart inside out if I hadn't still been dying to be with Stanley. Roger was fun, but I couldn't take him seriously, and I could tell he felt the same about me.

"Where did you learn to be such a good dancer?" he asked.

I told him the story of the community education

ballroom dance class, and about my grandma's cliff-hanger of a return to her golden wedding anniversary party after her trip to the South American jungle. Roger thought that was a riot.

Since we weren't genuine dates, we changed partners often and I met some new people. Sonny wasn't as obnoxious to me now that I was his brother's partner. I kept looking for Stanley, and when I couldn't find him, I asked Daphne what had happened to him.

"DeeDee couldn't come," she told me. "She had some kind of an eye infection. Her eye was all red and puffy and she was embarrassed to go out."

It was kind of a relief that Stanley wasn't coming. It would be too hard to see him with someone else.

When the dance ended, Daphne approached me with Étienne.

"Meg!" she exclaimed. "You and Étienne haven't danced together. I know you'll enjoy his French style of rock 'n' roll."

Étienne had longish, curly black hair and ebony eyes. He was good-looking in a sharp, foxy sort of way, with a pointy nose and chin. He had a thick accent that was hard to understand. I tried out some of my French on him and he only looked bewildered. He was a very good dancer, and I enjoyed bopping around the floor with him until I saw something that shocked me so much that I tripped over his foot.

*"Pardon!"* He took the blame in his exotic French style, but I couldn't get back into step because of what

I saw. It was Stanley Stoneman arriving—but not alone. Latched onto his arm was the last person I'd ever expect to see with him. Katie Gneiss!

A hollow sensation grabbed my interior. It was my worst nightmare come true. I danced like a robot, my gaze fixed on Stanley. He was looking for a seat at one of the tables. How Katie had been invited to this ball, by Stanley, of all people, was beyond my imagination.

The dance ended. *"Merci, mademoiselle,"* Étienne said with a little nod.

Wally, Étienne's host, cruised by with Jennifer Ridley and I pulled Étienne toward them, wanting to be enclosed in a group so that Katie couldn't flaunt Stanley. Daphne had been dancing with Roger, and they gravitated to our little cluster, too. Daphne looked both radiant and mischievous. She gave me a glance and a gesture that told me she wanted to get together with me in the restroom to share some secret.

"I hope you won't think I'm horning in on your territory," she told me when we were safely away from the others. She gave me a best-friends smile. "But I am so entranced with Roger, and since this was just a blind date for you, and Étienne is so fascinating, do you mind if I kind of monopolize Roger, and let you entertain our French visitor? He ought to get to know more people besides me, and you have so many interests, I know you'll be a fun partner for him."

"It doesn't matter to me. You're welcome to Roger, even though I do like him. Sometimes I can't understand Étienne. My French isn't that great."

"To tell the truth, I can't communicate with him very well, either," Daphne agreed, "but it's okay with you if I'm attracted to Roger, then?"

"Of course. After all, you're the one who got this party up. You ought to have your choice. But since you're changing partners so often, I wondered if you had thought about Kent Whitehead lately. He's sort of—like they say in old movies—carrying a torch for you and feeling down."

Daphne looked startled to hear Kent's name. "Oh, you know, Meg, that was kind of a phase for me, and I thought it would be for him, too. You know—out of sight, out of mind. He'll get involved with someone else, like I have with Roger. Meg, I'm so lucky to have you for a friend."

I was marveling at Daphne's quick changes of affection when the door swung open and who should track me down but Katie Gneiss.

"I thought I saw you ducking in here," she exclaimed, a touch of triumph in her eyes. "I just wanted you to know how lucky it is that you and Stanley have broken up, and how it worked out for him and me. It was almost like magic." She shook her long blond hair back over her shoulder. "I had a call from Jeff, saying he'd sprained his back in a baseball game this afternoon, and it hurt so bad he wouldn't be able to go out tonight. So I'd heard a rumor about you and Stanley being finished, and I thought he might like to know how I was coming along on my science fair project. I dialed his number, and it was almost as if he'd been sitting there waiting for me to call. Before I even got a syllable out about my project, he goes, 'Are you doing anything tonight?'

"I go, 'Nothing I can't get out of,' and he goes, 'I have some tickets to the hospital auxiliary ball that I hate to waste. Interested?' So here I am, isn't that a lucky coincidence?"

I was chilled to my core. What had happened to Stanley to make him give in to such an impulse? Bringing Katie to the ball was totally out of character. He must be badly stressed out. How had I messed things up with him? Why had I made him go to those stupid parties? Why had I asked him to be nice to Thelma and help Brian with his physics? If it had been just Stanley and me, the arrogant Katie wouldn't be gloating over me. Worse yet, Stanley was in danger. There was no telling, now that Katie had her claws into him, what she'd do to him. She'd have him hanging out at committee meetings, and would make him give up such impractical activities as trying to find out what was inside of a comet or what was the best kind of vehicle to travel on the surface of Mars. She'd never understand him, she'd ruin him. She'd refuse to ride in his homemade car and influence him to get a sports car. It was outrageous that he should have come here with her.

"Who is that sexy guy you're with?" she asked. "I don't remember seeing him around."

"He's from Paris," I said. "An exchange student at Broxton Academy. He's probably waiting for me.

Nice to see you." How could I be so cool when I was seething inside? Anyway, Katie looked properly impressed by my French connection.

I felt broken up in little fragments. Humptydumptyish? I knew that Étienne, who was still alone when I came out, thought I was a total dork, because I couldn't concentrate. I tried not to look at Stanley and Katie, and yet my eyes were drawn to them. Katie had on an electric blue dress and her hair shone like brass above it. Stanley had kind of a numb look. I saw them approaching Mr. and Mrs. Stoneman, and Katie almost falling over them in her effort to make an impression. She had on too much mascara for Mrs. Stoneman, I was sure. Katie's father was the head of the Board of Education in Hillview, and she would find a way to inform the Stonemans of that. She'd parade some ancestor before Mrs. Stoneman to prove she was a better girlfriend than I was for Stanley. After all I'd been through to get Mrs. Stoneman to like me, it was rotten to have Katie telling her that she was president of the junior class at Hillview.

In a dreamlike procession, Étienne danced with Jennifer Ridley and I found myself with Wally Urquhart, who was eventually replaced by Sonny Whitlow. Daphne kept a tight rein on Roger, and when the dance with Sonny ended, he maneuvered us toward Stanley and Katie. I saw the whirl of electric blue before me and smelled a whiff of Vampire perfume, and suddenly I was face to face with the dreaded couple.

"So, Stoneman!" Sonny kept his arm around me. I remembered that there was some old leftover childhood rivalry simmering in Sonny that drew him to go after any girl in whom Stanley seemed to be interested. Now, while letting Stanley know that he had me in his possession, I could see him making eyes at Katie.

"Trade you," he said with his toothy grin.

Stanley didn't respond, so Sonny reached for Katie's hand. "Whitlow," he introduced himself, since Stanley evidently wasn't going to do so.

"Katie, Katie Gneiss." She sort of squealed out her name in a voice that was too high-pitched. Her eyes flashed the message at me that she'd not only grabbed one guy from me, but a second.

The orchestra had rearranged their music on their stands, and they embarked on a tango. Stanley made no move to dance. He just glared at me.

"I didn't come with Sonny Whitlow, if that's what you're thinking," I said. "But you finally gave in to that Katie Gneiss."

"It's all your fault."

"Oh, I'm sure! I heard she just happened to dial your phone and you lost no time in asking her here."

"You goaded me into it. I knew you'd be here with somebody, worming your way into the Broxton crowd."

"This party was organized by our candy stripers to raise money for the hospital," I said. "That's the only reason I'm here."

"You said you hated that sleaze Sonny."

"You said Katie was the most irritating person you'd ever known."

"Which shows how you loused me up. You only went around with me to get in with this crowd."

"You know that's a lie. Daphne just sold tickets to the Urquharts so they could take the French exchange student, who came with Daphne, only Daphne has sort of dropped him for Roger, which is the only reason you found me with Sonny."

"Typical, a bunch of shallow people trying to amuse themselves with a new person every couple of hours," Stanley said.

"What about yourself? All you are now is a feather in Katie's cap. She'll spread it all over town that you invited her to this big dance. What do you think Jeff Hanford is going to say about that?"

The orchestra was playing "Jealousy," one of the songs Stanley and I had learned to tango by.

"Suitable music for the occasion," Stanley said.

"Who's jealous?" I asked, though I knew the answer to that question—me. I swallowed a big lump in my throat and went back to my table before Stanley could see I still cared.

8

Lee Ann and I got together at school on Monday.

"Even Stanley's tutoring hasn't put Brian on the B honor roll," Lee Ann complained to me. "He claims he freezes when he's taking a test, and even when he knows things, he can't put them down right. I told him to talk to Stanley about it, and Stanley told him he was no shrink."

"So Stanley is still working with Brian," I said.

"Oh, yes. He even takes Brian to his lab so he can see how it all works. He tells Brian it should be fun, kind of like a game, and he says that ought to cure him of his fear of physics."

I envied Brian going out to Stanley's new lab, which I hadn't even seen. I had only visited him at his old lab, which had burned down.

"Brian talked to the orchestra leader, but all he said was that rules were rules, and anyone who didn't have the grade point average didn't go to Tokyo. We don't even dare talk about the trip like we used to."

Lee Ann wasn't the only one of my friends who was stressed out. Kent Whitehead was still suffering about Daphne, and I could no longer pretend to him that she'd get in touch with him again. Daphne had told me after the benefit ball that Roger Whitlow had invited her to go to UCLA for a weekend. Daphne had applied to UCLA for the next year. "Then I'll get to see Roger every day," she said. She hadn't been so enthusiastic about anyone since I'd known her.

As much as I liked Daphne, I didn't think she should leave so many wounded ex-boyfriends in her wake, especially ones as vulnerable as Kent. When Daphne had been interested in him, he'd blossomed into a more talkative and relaxed person, but now he was going back into his shell, turning shy and uncommunicative again. I tried to befriend him, because I'd known him so long, probably longer than any other boy in school.

I continued my campaign to get him interested in someone else. "So if you aren't dating Daphne anymore, find another girlfriend," I said. "A lot of the girls around school would be very flattered if a basketball star like you would pay attention to them. You're a good-looking guy, and you should be out having fun instead of moping around about an ex-girlfriend."

"I'll never like anyone as much as Daphne. Nobody could ever be as beautiful as she is. Besides, I wasn't a basketball star this season. I didn't even get to play because of my broken leg. So who'd notice me?"

While I was trying to boost Kent's spirits, I noticed Stanley watching us from down the hall, and when he caught my eye, he turned and hurried away. He had always been suspicious of Kent, because I'd invited him to my grandparents' golden wedding anniversary party. No matter how many times I'd assured Stanley that I wasn't interested in Kent, he became wary whenever Kent came into the picture. Why should it matter to him now?

Katie Gneiss continued to pursue Stanley. For some unfathomable reason, he hadn't shaken her off. The week after the hospital benefit ball, there was a big ruckus in the school plaza. Some electrifying violence took place when Jeff Hanford, Katie's old boyfriend, caught Katie with Stanley. There was a flash of Jeff's muscular arm, and although Stanley doesn't have a belligerent nature, he put up his fists to defend himself, and the two were soon brawling on the pavement, with a delighted Katie looking on. I wanted to go over and have it out with her for forcing Stanley into a fight, telling her off once and for all. But I didn't have a chance to get into it, because the assistant principal's whistle sounded and the fighters were torn apart and hauled into the office for disciplining.

Katie couldn't resist crowing at me. Her eyes glinted with a kind of unpleasant power, so I just walked away from her. I was afraid she had destroyed something precious. Had she changed Stanley into somebody else? Had my old Stanley been erased forever?

Thelma appeared at the very end of the fracas. "What was that all about?" she asked.

"Maybe a front-page story for the school paper," I answered. "Jeff Hanford lights into Stanley Stoneman for stealing his girlfriend."

Thelma's face took on a stricken look. "This is all my fault, isn't it? When I went to the old car show with Stanley, it spoiled things between you and left him fair game for Katie."

"Quit blaming yourself, Thelma. You had nothing to do with that Katie thing."

"Can't you make him come to his senses? If you want to, that is. Like I told you before, I've decided— for myself—that guys aren't worth bothering about. All they cause is grief."

"They probably think the same thing about girls," I said, for I could see Kent Whitehead down the hall, his shoulders collapsed, slumping over his load of books. "Take Kent, for instance. He's suffering from being rejected by Daphne Wainwright."

"He was doomed from the start," Thelma commented. "She's way too high-powered for a guy like Kent."

"She thought he was okay," I said. "He's matured a lot in the last few months."

Thelma shrugged.

"Do you want to meet for lunch?" I asked.

"I have too much to do," she said. "I'm going into the journalism room and finish an article for the paper. I brought an apple with me."

"You ought to get a respectable lunch," I scolded. "You're working too hard and losing a lot of weight."

"I know." She pulled the waistband of her slacks out and I could see that there was room enough for another half a Thelma in there.

"But I have to work hard. What kind of life will I have if I don't get appointed editor next year? Everything else in my life has collapsed. The doctors still aren't sure if they got all the cancer out of my dad or not. It's like we're walking on eggs at home. We don't know what's going to happen. The only thing I have any control over is my grades and my newspaper work. Nothing else."

"Relax, Thelma. You write more and better articles for the paper than anyone else."

"Nobody can afford to rest on her laurels," Thelma said. "Incidentally, my article about the juvenile detention program went over big with Miss Wagstaff, and I also got a note from the principal complimenting me on writing an article informing my fellow students of the consequences of irresponsible behavior. Those were his exact words."

"You're good, Thelma," I said. She needed recreation as well as ego building, and I suggested that she and Lee Ann and I get together on Sunday afternoon. Lee Ann said she would be glad to come because Brian was going to Stanley's lab that day.

"Brian says Stanley is always talking about you, Meg," she told me when we were at my house, sitting on the floor in my room. We made each other up and squirted ourselves with various perfumes. Then we got on our roller skates and went to a paved area in the park and acted crazy. We even had Thelma being silly again.

I kept thinking of Brian's remark that Stanley mentioned me often. It was stupid for us to be avoiding each other. I was probably more aggressive than Stanley. I should be the one to make the move, and I would if I wasn't so bummed out about his taking Katie to the ball. I hadn't seen her since the fracas with Jeff. In fact, I hadn't seen Stanley at all recently.

When we were on our way home from the park with our roller skates around our necks, Brian overtook us on his bike. He got off, put his helmet on the back, and walked along beside us.

"I heard you've been to the lab," I said.

"It was pretty lonesome. Stanley is out of town. He was asked to display that weird Martian puddle jumper, or whatever he calls it, at a science fair in San

Diego. Did you ever hear of such luck? He's not only going to get out of school all week to tell other schools about his invention, but they pay his way. He makes such good grades that nobody cares whether he comes to school or not. Me, if I take even a day off, I'm in danger of flunking."

"You're exaggerating," Lee Ann said. "You told me you were improving in physics."

"I did," Brian said. "But now my other subjects are slipping. I'm about fifty pages behind in social studies. There's just not enough of me to go around." Brian made a comical face and scrunched down to make himself even smaller than he was. We all laughed.

Thelma lectured Brian about keeping his grades up. "What you have to do is read all the directions in the book. Then you do your work, and afterward, check it. If you're that careful, you can't miss. You have to give it your best. Going to Tokyo is a once-in-a-lifetime chance. I wish I'd get an offer like that, only they haven't asked for an exchange of newspaper staffs over there."

"Yeah, you can give advice, because you get almost as good grades as Stoneman," Brian said.

"But I don't do it easily, like he does," Thelma said. "I have to work at it."

"Brian has got to make that concert," Lee Ann said. "It won't be worthwhile for me if he doesn't go. The whole year will be a total loss."

Brian took her hand, guiding his bike with the

other. I wished Stanley and I had had a smooth relationship like that. I could never imagine Brian and Lee Ann getting into a quarrel or breaking up.

What was the use of thinking about Stanley? He wasn't there, and Thelma, who needed me to think about her, was with me. Our friendship had been on shaky ground a while ago. It was lucky I had time for Thelma, because later that week she needed a lot of support.

Just as the Arkadians thought Thelma's father was on the mend, he had a relapse, with serious complications. I was at the hospital and called Thelma right away. I offered to go over and stay at her house and answer the phone, feed the cat, or whatever.

Mrs. Arkadian and Thelma weren't gone long though. I didn't have to ask if everything was okay. One look at Thelma's face and I realized that it wasn't.

"We didn't get there in time," Mrs. Arkadian said, her voice flat.

Thelma's look was tormented and I realized what had happened.

Thelma nodded and the tears gushed and she and her mother and I all put our arms around one another and just stood there in a kind of limbo, not believing such a thing could happen in these familiar surroundings.

Mrs. Arkadian asked me if I'd make a few phone calls. She couldn't get her voice to behave. I called one of Thelma's sisters, who said she'd call the other one.

After a while people began arriving—uncles and aunts, friends, the pastor. A doctor came, too, and gave Thelma and her mother something to calm them, and I slipped away home.

Dad was just arriving home from work at his print shop. His arrival was usually just a routine occurrence, but that day, just the sight of him filled me with so much relief and joy that I rushed to hug him. "Oh, you're here, Dad!" I exclaimed.

Since I don't usually greet him with such feeling, he looked pleasantly surprised.

"Why, honey, of course. It's almost dinnertime," he said.

"I love you, Dad," I burst out. My dad and I don't usually make such statements out of the blue, and he said, "Is everything all right? You're not in any kind of trouble, Meg?"

"Daddy, I'm just glad to be with you, and that you're okay."

"Why wouldn't I be okay? I didn't run into any unusual hazards at work or on the way home. It's just a routine day. Something's on your mind, Megan. There's something you want to talk about. Is it money? New sneakers, or a new jacket? Just let me get my coat off, and get something cold to drink, and we'll talk."

"Let me get you some iced tea," I said. "And just sit down and take it easy."

As soon as we were comfortable out on the patio, I said, "I just suddenly realized how lucky I am to have a healthy dad who's right here with me. It means a lot to me, Dad."

Then finally I told him about Mr. Arkadian, and he said he and my mom would see what they could do to help out.

"Dad," I continued, "you and I should spend more time together. I just realized how important it is for people as close as a father and daughter to make the most of the time they have together. I feel so sorry for Thelma," I said, tears spilling down my cheeks.

"It's going to be hard for her," Dad said. "She'll need a lot of support, and this is a time when your friendship will mean a lot to her. But don't worry about your old dad, Meg. I'm hale and hearty and you and I are going to have lots of time together. I know I've been working a lot of long hours, honey, but I hope to hire another assistant soon, and then you'll have me underfoot more than you may like."

"That would be great, Dad," I said.

# 9 ～

I WAS THE ONE who had to tell Thelma's friends about her dad's death. I also reported to Miss Wagstaff and the school administration that she wouldn't be at school for a few days.

When I told Kent Whitehead, he seemed especially sympathetic.

"Should I do something? Send her a card or anything? She's been so nice to me. She wrote me up for the school paper, remember?"

"A card would help."

"You want to help me pick one out?"

"Sure," I said. "Maybe I'll get one myself. We can go to the drugstore after school."

At the store Kent picked a card that had a picture of some birds on the front and said nothing inside. "I'll write something," he said. "That's better than sending a canned message. It'll have more meaning."

Kent decided to take his card to Thelma's instead of mailing it. I could see that he was changing from a self-conscious kid into a thoughtful guy. Not that I could ever get romantically interested in Kent. How could I, since Stanley had come into my life? If I couldn't have Stanley, no one would do.

The next time I saw her Thelma told me that Kent's visit had helped. I asked her when she was coming back to school. "It's too lonely here," I said, gesturing around the empty house. Her older sisters had gone back to college, and her mom returned to work. "You'll feel better at school."

"I don't feel like going back yet," she said.

I talked to Lee Ann about Thelma. "We have to do something to help her," I said. "We're her best friends."

"It's going to be a major effort to pry her out of her house."

We set off for Thelma's after I grabbed the latest issue of the Hillview *Howl* and put it in my tote bag. When she opened the door and saw us she gave a ghost of a smile.

"Come out and get a Coke with us," Lee Ann suggested.

Thelma withdrew. "Not right now," she said. "You can come in if you want," she said in a listless tone.

"We wondered when you're coming back to school," I said when we were seated.

Thelma seemed to resent that question, which maybe I'd asked her too often. "When I feel like it," she said.

"You'd better not stay away too long," I scolded. "Wait till you see what's happening to the *Howl* now that you're not there to spark it up. There are none of your funny personality sketches of kids around school. It's all just boring information. Like, 'The French Club met on Wednesday and decided to change its meeting day to Thursday,' or 'The following were chosen at tryouts for the cast of *Kismet,* the annual school musical,' and a list of names. If you'd been writing you would have described those actors and told interesting things about them and how they got their roles."

Thelma snatched the paper from me with the first spark of interest I'd seen in her since her father died. The spark was kindled as she scanned the paper. "I sure would have," she said. She slammed the paper down on the table with an expression of disgust. "It looks like Turner Spivey has taken over," she said. "And I can see Wanda Zetterquist's touch here in all this drivel: 'What sophomore cutie is on the verge of fascinating a certain player on the school tennis team?' Who cares?"

"See, everybody misses your stories," Lee Ann said.

"The paper looked skimpy this week," I said. "It's time for you to come back."

The glow died away in Thelma's eyes. "I wouldn't be any use to them—I don't have the same drive I used to have," she said. "They're putting out the paper without me. It's time to pick next year's editor, and I'll be totally out of the running, because I think I've lost whatever inspired me."

"Don't be a pessimist, Thelma. You'll get your old zip back as soon as you get back in the *Howl* newsroom."

Thelma just gave one of her hopeless shrugs, and Lee Ann changed the subject by telling about some funny tricks Brian had played on the members of the orchestra. "Besides that," she added, "Brian has been fooling around with Stanley Stoneman, and guess what? He's trying to invent a new kind of musical instrument. It's called a trombophone." She laughed. "What a weird gadget. I doubt if the orchestras of the world will adopt it."

Thelma reacted with a smile to that, but she was fidgeting in her chair, and I sensed we were making her nervous, and she wished we would go.

"We'd better go now, but I'll phone you tonight," I said.

Thelma didn't urge us to stay, but I felt our visit had helped a bit.

On the way home I said to Lee Ann, "I'm really worried about her. She ought to get back to school. Let's call her twice a day to see if she's okay and keep up our campaign to get her back to school."

It wasn't easy for me to check on Thelma because I

was so busy. The next afternoon I had to go to the candy stripers. It was almost a relief to be with Daphne Wainwright, who was always happy and full of energy. On that particular day, Daphne was on a high because she'd received a couple of college acceptances. One of them was from her number-one choice, UCLA.

She sang out the news to me, whirling around until her pinafore caught the current of her movement. "Imagine, every day I can walk to classes with Roger. I phoned him and he was thrilled that I'd be coming there next year. He said he'd show me around."

Hearing Daphne's college news, I realized that Stanley must also be receiving acceptances from colleges.

After my conversation with Daphne, I rushed upstairs to check on the premature babies for my report.

Dr. Hummel was there, and I asked him if he'd look at the material I had gathered so far, the statistics I had assembled as a possible entry in the science fair. Dr. Hummel took me into his office and sat down at his cluttered desk.

"This is quite complete information on the babies you've included in your study. I'm delighted that you've chosen to interest yourself in the subject. However, if you wish to make a significant entry in the science fair, you need to have more subjects." He looked over my drawings, which showed the tubes and wires attached to the babies, and explained how they told the staff what was happening to the infants in the incubators, and how some of them helped the babies to stay alive. He corrected the spelling of one of the words.

"You mean I need more babies?" I asked. "But how could I? These four are the only ones who have survived in the nursery since I started keeping records."

Dr. Hummel smiled at me, his Santalike face crinkling with kindness. "Research isn't something we rush to a deadline, Megan. Keep at it, and eventually —next year, maybe—you'll have enough infants in your study to draw some conclusions."

"Next year!" I exclaimed. "But the science fair is almost here. My science teacher already gave me an A on this as a term paper."

"You've done a nice, neat, careful job on your project. I'm sure you deserve an A. Perhaps I'm too exacting, considering that this is a high school fair. I'm afraid I'm treating you like a professional."

"That's okay, Dr. Hummel. I didn't expect this was anything great. It's just something I'm interested in." Actually, I was flattered that he thought of me as a professional. I got the message that there were things in the world more important than the science fair.

"Keep up your interest, Megan, and you'll make a fine pediatrician." Dr. Hummel handed the folder back to me.

"I hope you'll let me keep observing any new preemies who come in. I may decide not to enter this in the science fair if you think it's too scanty."

"That's up to you. I'm not an expert on school science fairs, so I can't judge your project as an entry."

"Basically, I'm doing this for my future career, not to enter the science fair, Dr. Hummel. I guess it was contagious when I saw the other kids in school entering it, and I wanted to be in on the action."

"That's understandable." Dr. Hummel rummaged among the papers on his desk and I got the idea that he was too busy to talk to me any longer.

"Thanks for all your help," I said. It always made me feel very mature to talk to Dr. Hummel. "I'd better report back to the candy stripers."

Back on duty I ran into DeeDee Banfield, whom I had not seen in weeks—since before the ball.

"Too bad you had a problem that kept you from the ball," I said.

"I felt bad about leaving Stanley and his family in the lurch. His mother was pretty upset with me that I opted out when I had promised to come. Mainly, I think, because he showed up with some girl she couldn't stand. Do you know who she was?"

I turned my full attention on DeeDee. "Katie Gneiss. A girl from Hillview."

"Mrs. Stoneman didn't approve of her at all. She told my mother she didn't know how Stanley ever took up with such a pushy, ostentatious girl."

"No kidding!" I exclaimed.

"Mrs. Stoneman told mother that this Katie whoever had a bad influence on Stanley, that he was irritable and touchy all the time, and she wished he'd kept going out with you. He seemed to be so much more steady and contented then. Just thought I'd pass that along. This girl must have been some kind of a motor-mouth. I heard that she spent the whole time bragging about herself and how important she was, president of this or that, how many dates she had, and how lucky it was that this football player happened to be sick or something, which was the only reason she was able to go to the ball, since she was usually booked up for days."

"I wonder if Stanley went out with her again after that night?" I asked.

"I think she must have been heckling him, because Mrs. Stoneman complained to my mother that this Katie simply would not leave him alone. Apparently she calls him up all the time and Stanley's mother said she drove out to their house to track Stanley down at this little outbuilding where he likes to putter. She said Stanley happened to be out of town at the time, so she sent the gardener out to get that girl off the premises. How come you quit going with Stanley, anyway, Meg?"

The news of Katie going out to Stanley's lab shook me. I didn't want her to know where it was, even. That had been our special place.

"It was just a stupid disagreement, DeeDee. I wish it hadn't happened, if you want to know the truth. But he's stubborn, and I'm afraid I am, too. I don't know how to patch things up."

"Well, hey, Meg," DeeDee added. "I hope you don't think I was out to get Stanley, or anything. The arrangement for me to go to the ball with him was set up. I like Stanley, but I'm kind of committed to Richard Farwell. I was free that night, because Richard had gone away on a trip with his dad. I hope you two get back together."

"No, I didn't think anything about you going to the ball with Stanley, DeeDee," I assured her. "I was in the same kind of a deal myself. Filling in for someone who had bought a ticket and needed a date."

"I hope you had a good time, anyway."

"Sure. It was okay. I went with Daphne and that French exchange student and some other people. Nobody was exactly on a date."

# *10* ~

I HEARD ABOUT Katie's visit to Stanley's lab for a second time when Lee Ann and Brian stopped by my house. They gave me a cautious look, and then glanced at each other with secret messages in their eyes.

Lee Ann said, "Tell her, Brian."

My nerves came alert for bad news.

Brian cleared his throat a couple of times. His usually smiling face turned serious, and slightly red.

"Lee and I knew something had gone wrong between you and Stanley and we've discovered what it is," Brian said.

"Katie Gneiss," Lee Ann said, her lip curling with scorn.

"Tell me something I don't already know," I said.

"She seems to be taking him over," Brian protested. "See, even though I knew Stanley was out of town one day, I needed to do some work on this musical instrument I'm thinking of entering in the science fair."

"The trombophone," Lee Ann said proudly. "Can you imagine that Brian is going to be in the science fair?"

"Stanley said it was okay for me to use his lab, even when he wasn't there, because I needed to use his equipment to finish my project. So I was out there, buffing the outside of the trombophone, when what should pull up beside the lab but Katie's Fiat. She was hot on Stanley's trail. Right away, some servant came and told Katie that Stanley wasn't home and she should leave. Neither she nor the servant saw me, because I came on my bike and it and I were inside. Anyway, Katie seemed to be scared of the servant, and she turned around and left. Can you imagine her tracking him clear out to his house? She'll stop at nothing to nail the guy."

"She's always hanging around him now," Lee Ann added. "We figured that she was the one who broke up you and Stanley, and you shouldn't take it."

"She's bad for Stanley," Brian said. "He's always moody now. You know what she's heckled him into doing? Rigging up a watering system for that stupid entry of hers in the science fair."

"She has about as much interest in science as I do," Lee Ann said. "She only entered the fair so she could hang around him."

In spite of my intense anger, I wanted to appear cool, as if Katie couldn't get to me. "So what?" I shrugged.

"Meg, you and Stanley are meant to be together. There's no couple around Hillview who were better suited as partners. You can't let Katie ruin that," Brian said. "I guess it was partly my fault that she came out to Stanley's, because she asked how I had gotten to be such close friends with him. I told her I was working in his lab and I'm afraid that gave her the idea where she could stalk him after school."

"She has so much gall," Lee Ann added. "You ought to tell her off, Meg."

"I'm not so sure I want to," I said. "If Stanley is stupid enough to fall for Katie's tricks, he deserves her. Besides, he took her to the hospital ball, so he must like her."

"No, he doesn't," Brian said stubbornly. "He misses you, Meg. I think that's how Katie got to him. He needs you. You have to go back to him and save him from Miss Egotist."

"He's the one who started it. Let him be the one who comes back—if he can escape from Katie, which I doubt."

The process of hearing about Katie and Stanley

hurt so much that I hoped I'd never see Stanley again. Let him accept his invitation from MIT so I wouldn't have to hear any more about him. I resented Brian and Lee Ann, too, for telling me to get Stanley back from Katie. Why didn't someone bug him to get me back? Why did I have to be responsible?

"I need to do some homework," I said.

"Remember what we said. Stick up for your rights," Lee Ann said. "Oh, incidentally, I talked to Thelma today, and I think she might be coming back to school. She seems to be weakening."

"I'll give her another nudge," I promised.

I started to do my homework, but I was too restless. I needed to talk to someone, but not anyone who knew too much about Stanley and Katie. I didn't want to hear any more about them. I ended by dialing Daphne Wainwright's number, to get off on a different subject.

Daphne was her usual bubbly self. She was eager to tell me that Roger Whitlow was coming up from UCLA to take her sailing on Sunday. "Meg, why don't you go with us?" she suddenly burst out. "The sailboat belongs to Roger's roommate. We could make it a foursome. He doesn't know any girls up here. They asked me to get a girl for him, and I was about to call DeeDee. But I couldn't get ahold of her. I left my number on her answering machine. Now that you're on the phone, you can be the one. Have you been sailing? Neither have I. This will be a blast!"

I made a quick decision to go. Why keep moping

about Stanley? I'd show him! I'd meet new people. I'd go out sailing with Roger's roommate, learn something new, and have fun doing it.

"What's his name?" I asked Daphne.

"Oliver Trimble," Daphne said. "Roger already knows you, and he'll tell Oliver what a neat person you are, so it won't exactly be a blind date. Listen, let's hang up, and I'll call Roger and get it all set up. Then I'll call you back and let you know what time we're leaving and all that."

Daphne couldn't make a connection with Roger until about midnight, and she woke up my entire family calling back. "Those phones in the college dorms are always busy," she complained. "But once I reached him, he said, great, he'd be looking forward to having you along. We'll be leaving at eleven o'clock on Sunday morning, and of course, those guys, living in a dorm, expect us to bring some food. Come over early? We'll make some sandwiches, and they'll pick us up here."

It felt strange to be going out with another college guy. Basically, I'm pretty inexperienced. Stanley is the only guy I've been out with, or wanted to, unless you count a couple of minor excursions with Kent and Dennis Ridge, and, of course, that half a date with Roger. Stanley was always such an easy, uncomplicated person to be with, until we started arguing. How would I adapt to this mature sailor? But going sailing with him seemed a good thing to do in my present, antsy mood.

When Sunday arrived I found that Oliver Trimble was a sort of heavyset guy wearing a perpetual smile under a sailor hat that was pushed down over his eyebrows, so I couldn't see exactly what he looked like. He wore a red windbreaker with a zipper pull that was shaped like an anchor. A good-natured guy, he was always laughing and chuckling.

He was careful to see that I was okay, when we were on the boat, watching me like a hawk so I wouldn't be socked on the head by this heavy horizontal bar that moved when the wind caught the sails.

"You feel okay, don't you?" he occasionally asked me. "Not feeling squeamish, are you? Pretty choppy water today, but I hope it isn't bothering you." Eventually, the briny, fishy smell of the bay and the rhythmic swells of the water, and of course, Oliver's suggestions that I might be getting seasick made his fears come true. I began to wish that the sailboat would sink and put me out of my misery.

"We better take you back to the dock," Oliver finally said. He turned the sailboat back to deposit me on the pier. Daphne was enjoying sailing, and she wasn't affected by the waves, so she went on with the guys, leaving me to watch the gulls swooping in and perching on the railings until my churning tummy stabilized.

When the other three returned, Oliver apologized for the rough water. "I'll take you out to dinner to make up for it," he said. "How about it, Roger, Daphne?"

"Terrific," Daphne said. "But we'll have to go home and change."

"I'm not sure I feel like dinner," I said.

"Oh, sure you do. You missed out on the sail, so you ought to get a consolation prize," Daphne said.

"Call me after I get home and I'll let you know how I feel," I said. Daphne, I could tell, thought I was a party pooper. She'd probably never ask me anyplace else.

I didn't really want to go. It wasn't fun going out with anyone except Stanley. I knew I should forget him, that we were finished, and I should try going with someone else.

But then I felt a surge of anger about being separated from Stanley, and when we passed Hillview High on my way home, it was even more disconcerting to see a couple of guys hanging a sign in front of school: Katie Gneiss for Student Body President.

Katie was conspicuous everywhere. She wanted to run everything, to win everything, to have everything. I couldn't get over being amazed that Stanley had fallen into her trap. I made a resolution that the next day at school I'd offer to pass out leaflets for Dirk Wilkins, who was running in the election against Katie.

My dad answered the phone that evening when Oliver called to see if I wanted to go to dinner. The phone never rang that I didn't hope it was Stanley, calling to make up with me and say that everything was the way it used to be. Even though I expected Oliver to call, his voice was disappointing. My immediate reaction was to say, "No."

I tried to be tactful. "You picked the wrong person to take on a sailing trip," I said. "I'm afraid my appetite hasn't returned and I still have sea legs. I'll have to beg off for tonight."

"Too bad," Oliver said, "because this is the only night I'll be here."

"Maybe one of Daphne's other friends can go," I said. "Anyway, I enjoyed meeting you, and thanks for the experience of sailing, even though it didn't work out."

After I hung up, my dad said, "I didn't recognize that fellow's voice. You have a new boyfriend? What happened to Stanley?"

"I don't see him anymore," I said. I felt a lump rise in my throat and that restless feeling overtook me again.

Dad tweaked my ponytail teasingly. "These cases of puppy love come and go," he said.

Dad didn't realize how serious this situation was. Puppy love! I couldn't believe he could apply those words to Stanley and me.

But he just winked at me. "It's time to give some of these other boys a chance. A pretty girl shouldn't waste her youth sitting home moping."

I tried to get my dad to be more serious, appealing to his sympathy by telling him how I'd been seasick, and he just got a laugh out of that.

"Nothing seems like fun unless Stanley is with me," I said.

Dad shrugged and went over to his desk to unzip his briefcase. "It'll take a new boyfriend to convince you otherwise," he said.

I had hoped my dad could tell me something about how to get Stanley back. It takes a guy to know a guy, right? But he wasn't about to take me seriously, so I escaped to my grandma's. She's always ready to hash over my problems.

I went through the whole can of worms: the disastrous sailing trip, Katie's capture of Stanley, and my unhappiness without him.

Grandma pursed her lips and gave me a stern look and pretty much the same advice my dad had given me. "You're going to have to get your mind off Stanley if he keeps making you miserable. I'm surprised that Stanley would take up with this other girl. It's not like him."

"It's partly my fault, Grandma. I made him go to parties he didn't want to go to, and made him mix with some kids from his old social crowd. I should have listened to him and done what he wanted to do."

"No, Meg, you can't let him have his way all the time, and if he won't give an inch, you'll have to give some other boy a break. What about that tall boy we see in church who's always seeking you out?"

"Kent Whitehead! You always bring him up, Grandma. He just hangs around me to find out what's doing with Daphne. She made a big play for him and gave him the impression she liked him, and then this French exchange student came along and she dumped him. Now she's dumped the exchange student, too."

"So that does leave Kent available. . . ."

I knew she was about to mention her former yard boy, Dennis, so I repeated, "I can't have fun with anyone except Stanley."

"You're just as stubborn as I am. You got that one-track mind from me," Grandma said. "So I'm the one to tell you what to do. You have to get Stanley back."

"But how? And I don't know if I want him back if he's changed, if he's become one of Katie Gneiss's clones, if he's not the same as he was when he and I had our own special world."

"Be positive, Meg. Relax. If you quit fretting about Stanley, he just might come back to you. And even though this Whitehead boy has been 'dumped' as you say, couldn't you spend some time cheering up an old friend? You can never do too much of that."

Grandma looked over my head, and relief swept away the worry lines my problems had brought to her forehead. "I think I see a couple of your friends coming up to your house," she said.

# 11 ～

I PUSHED ASIDE the curtain and saw Lee Ann and Brian going up to the front door of my house. They were on roller skates and were in silly moods, bopping each other back and forth across the sidewalk. Brian's dog, Squirrelbait, frolicked behind them.

"Hey, Meg!" Brian yelled when I came out Grandma's door, "We're spreading the good news. I'm in! I made it for the Tokyo trip."

"Congratulations."

"Actually, Stanley deserves the congratulating."

"Or, you might say," Lee Ann interjected, "Meg does. She's the one who suggested that Stanley coach you."

"Whatever—I'm a happy guy!" Brian sat on the steps to take off his skates, and I could smell an aroma of popcorn clinging to him. His bright, curly hair shone in the sun. He looked up at me with a radiant smile.

"Mr. Giacomo phoned me at home. Even though it's Sunday, he had made up his final list and wanted everyone on it to know. He got grades from all our teachers early so he'd know who was going."

"If you hadn't got Stanley Stoneman on my case, I'd have been left behind for sure. The guy is not only a genius, but he can also show others how to stop being idiots. Do you think I'd ever have entered the science fair, or that I'd have had the idea of inventing a new instrument if Stanley hadn't helped me? I had to make my entry in such a hurry that it's pretty crude. But anyway, I showed it to Mr. Giacomo, and he said the music department was thrilled to be represented. My physics teacher thought it was so unusual to have a project on sound that he raised my grade. He says I won't win, but who cares? It's a miracle I'm in it."

"It's all because of you that Brian got inspired, passed the course, and is going on the trip. Thanks." Lee Ann hugged me. "Our only regret is that you and Stanley aren't going together anymore."

"I intend to get on Stanley's case about breaking up with you," Brian said. He changed the subject again. "Imagine, the worst loser in the science department, entered in the science fair, along with Stanley Stoneman."

"And Katie Gneiss," Lee Ann said, with a meaningful lift to one of her eyebrows. "She's making such a big thing of her entry you'd think she was about to win the Nobel prize. She goes around with this big gang of guys. One made a tray for her to display her fungus project in, another collected specimens for her, and she got someone from the art department to make a poster to explain it. She ought to be disqualified. I doubt if she did any of the work herself. I hope the judges can see how much more original work you've done on yours."

"I might not enter mine," I said.

"Not enter! But the science teacher used yours as an example of an innovative project. He thought it might win some kind of ribbon."

"I was talking to Dr. Hummel at the hospital, and he doubted that mine was ready. He says I need to do more research."

"You ought to stay in and give Katie's crummy project some competition," Brian said. "But of course, Stanley's will be the grand prize winner."

"Does Stanley have a fan, or what?" Lee Ann said.

"So it seems," I said. I knew they wondered how I could be so stupid as to let him go. But wasn't that just the point? That Stanley was such a strong individual he couldn't be held? So how could that shallow Katie Gneiss keep a hold on him? It was beyond belief, and I would have given anything to unroll the past, pour invisible ink over it, and start over again when Stanley and I were in the adult ed ballroom dancing class and he loved me.

We sat on the patio eating chocolate-chip cookies while Brian and Lee Ann entertained me with the Japanese phrases they'd learned for their trip. They were soaring.

When Brian and Lee Ann were back on their skates heading for home, my mom discovered that she was out of milk and asked me if I'd go to the store and pick some up.

Sprinting to the market, which was about a dozen blocks away, I came face to face with the gloomy figure of Kent Whitehead pulling up in the grocery parking lot in his dad's car.

"Hi, Kent." I waited for him outside the store.

Kent's mouth was set in a grim line as if it were frozen. Instead of smiling, he just nodded his head. His eyes were as sad as a spaniel's.

"Got to get some milk for my mom," I said as cheerfully as possible. "How you been?"

"Okay, I guess." Kent looked down at the ground, his shoulders drooping, but he managed to open the store door for me.

"How'd you like the assembly last Friday?" I had to keep drawing Kent out.

"Okay."

"Yeah, except for Gneiss's speech."

"You voting for Wilkins?"

"Sure. Are you?"

"Probably."

"What are you getting here?"

"Coffee. Bread."

I picked up the milk and trailed behind Kent, commenting on his purchases. "Don't pick that white bread. Grandma says bread with lots of fiber, the chewy kind, is better for you. Here."

Kent mutely accepted the bread I handed him. I knew he was still suffering from his rejection by Daphne Wainwright. Even though Daphne was my friend, I wished she could have figured that Kent wasn't the type of guy you could play games with. He'd taken her seriously, and now he was so hurt his ego had sort of dissolved away. I felt responsible, because I'd introduced Daphne and Kent. When I get to college, I'm going to take a course in psychology so I can help people like Kent get their egos back.

We were at the produce department. "Are these okay?" Kent pointed to some faintly streaked red apples. "Sometimes I choose mushy ones."

I approved the apples. When we had our purchases and had passed through the checkout counter, I asked, "Could I thumb a lift?"

"Sure," Kent said.

I felt in my jacket pocket where I had put a letter that Miss Wagstaff had asked me to deliver to Thelma as I was leaving school on Friday.

"Would you do me a favor?" I asked. "Could we make a small detour and go past Thelma's house? I just remembered I have something from school to give her."

"Sure," Kent agreed.

When I got out of the car, I said, "Why don't you come, too? She thought it was so nice when you brought her that card. It would cheer her up to see you."

Kent's face brightened just a shade. "I might as well," he said.

When Thelma came to the door, I could see she was even lower than Kent. Looking from her to Kent, I saw they reflected each other's moods perfectly.

"Hi, Thelma!" I tried to speak brightly. "Miss Wagstaff gave me a note to take to you. Some newspaper assignment, I guess. She wondered when you were coming back."

"I'm not sure."

She didn't invite us in, but I thought she needed company, so I elbowed my way through the door, dragging Kent behind me. "Kent and I ran into each other at the store. He was asking how you were, so we dropped by. How are things going?"

Thelma shrugged and closed the door behind us. She looked at the envelope I had brought her, then with a frown, slowly tore off one end. Kent and I watched from a standing position, because she hadn't asked us to sit down. She unfolded the letter and straightened it out. Her eyes came alive as they scanned the lines, some color appeared in her cheeks.

It was a changed Thelma who looked at us when she finished the letter. She grabbed each of us by the arm. "Wow!" she exclaimed as if someone had just set a lighted firecracker under her.

Kent's expression caught the mood and his mouth began to turn up at the corners. His eyes lit on the newly energized Thelma.

"Maybe you didn't know you were carrying the document appointing next year's editor of the Hillview *Howl!*" Thelma said, her head held at a high, proud angle, her eyes misted over. Even the lethargic Kent couldn't help giving a little yelp of triumph. "You deserve it," he exclaimed. "You wrote most of the good stories this year. I've been following them ever since you interviewed me. Before my leg got creamed."

"Next year, you'll be back on the court, and we'll interview you again."

Kent's sagging shoulders came to attention.

"Let's celebrate. I'll get some soda and chips, if that's gala enough," Thelma said. She went to the kitchen and came back with three Cokes and a bowl of chips.

"To the new editor!" I proposed.

"I didn't dream I'd get it. I thought either Turner or Wanda, or even Angie Calkins, would beat me out, especially with all that's happened to me recently. But that didn't throw Miss Wagstaff off. She says I'm to organize a basic staff to present to her for approval. Get that! I'm to pick the rest of the staff myself, and we're to get together during the summer to prepare an edition for the opening day of school next year. Turner is good. He can be news editor. Wanda will just die if she doesn't get some prominent position, so I'll call her features editor. The sports editor is graduating. I'll have to get a new one." She was silent awhile, thinking, darting little glances out of the corner of her eye at Kent.

"Have you ever taken journalism, Kent?"

"Nope."

"Maybe you could be guest editor for these last couple of weeks. This year's editor could brief you. You know all the guys and their skills, and all the sports lingo, and all that, don't you? Then you could sign up for journalism in your senior year and you could take over the regular job of sports editor."

Kent's eyes widened with amazement. He got up with his can of Coke, flourishing it in his hand as he paced in front of us. "I never thought of writing sports! Radical!" he exclaimed.

"Can I put you down, then?"

"Okay."

I couldn't believe the sudden transformation in Thelma and Kent.

"But I don't know a thing about writing for newspapers." He withdrew a little.

"You read them, don't you? The technique of newswriting is simple. You just put the most important facts in the first paragraph and keep putting in fewer and fewer crucial details so we can chop the story off if we don't have enough space. You're going to love it, Kent! We'll teach you to write headlines and captions for pictures, and how to proofread your page. It's great. And then you might end up being a sports reporter after you graduate. You'll have experience."

Kent stood there with a huge new world opening to him, while Thelma flitted to the phone, bristling with excitement. "I think I ought to let Lee Ann in on this, don't you? She'll want to know."

While Thelma punched in Lee Ann's number, Kent, his eyes narrowed with thought, kept pacing. "Do you think this is for real, Meg?"

"Sure. Thelma needs you. Just think about track meets. How big they are. They need lots of people to cover them. I can see the headline now. 'Hillview hurler sets discus record,' by Kent Whitehead."

Kent broke out in a grin and looked into the distance as if scanning the headline I had dreamed up. "You might not make a very good sportswriter," he remarked. "A hurler is usually thought of as a baseball pitcher."

Thelma chatted to Lee Ann. As she sat at the telephone, she pulled the drapes away from the window and a shaft of light illuminated the shadowy room. She pushed up the pane and a fresh breeze entered to mix with the musty air in the long-closed space.

I jumped up. "Hey, my mom is waiting for her milk. It'll get sour if I don't get home. You stay and talk to Thelma about your new job. I'll just slip out now."

On my way home I felt a warm glow, thinking about how Kent and Thelma had come alive. I told my mom about it when I reached home.

"The way Thelma and Kent were communicating, I wouldn't be surprised if they became an item. Thelma did like Kent once, only then he was boring, hard to talk to. She may find him more interesting now. And if they're working on the paper together, they'll have so much to talk about that Kent will probably turn into a motor-mouth."

"There's nothing like working on the same project to bring people together," my mom said. She told me about a couple at the hospital who worked together as lab technicians, and had become so attached that they were planning to be married.

I gave a big sigh. "Thelma and Kent will start going together, and even though I was the first of our group to date, now I'll be the only one who doesn't."

"Only because of your own stubbornness. Your dad tells me you turned down a fellow who wanted to take you out to dinner. And then there was that cute gardener, Dennis, who used to work at your grandma and grandpa's. He would have been a good boyfriend for you, but you had to discourage him. You'll have to overcome your infatuation for that Stanley. If you're left out of things, it's your own fault."

"Oh, Mom, this Oliver who wanted to go to dinner was only a blind date and he was only here for the day. And Dennis is ancient history."

"I can't say it often enough, Megan. You're too

young to think your first boyfriend has to be your last."

That was easy for my mom to say, but hard for me to swallow. I never stopped missing Stanley. I still felt guilty that I hadn't protected him from Katie Gneiss's manipulation. Katie was taking advantage of Stanley's newfound eagerness to help people. He had turned Brian Hotchkiss around, taught him skills that helped him bring his grades up to go to Tokyo. But Katie didn't need Stanley. She had other guys that she'd spirited away from other girls. She was only exploiting Stanley.

I almost blew my top the next day when she cornered me outside my English class.

"How's your science fair entry coming?" she asked.

"So-so," I mumbled, reluctant to give her any information, especially that I was still thinking of withdrawing.

"Mine is terrific." She flipped her blond hair over one shoulder and looked down the hall to identify some boy who was approaching. "I have eighteen specimens. You wouldn't believe how great Stanley has been. As you know, fungi require a lot of moisture. I was trying to figure out how to keep my collection from drying out while it's on display. Right away that great brain had the answer: 'Simple. Just put a trickle-and-drip system in the box.' 'Why I wouldn't begin to know how to do something like that,' I said. 'There's nothing to it,' he goes. He's just about got it rigged up. Of course, the water may have to be replaced once or twice during the fair, but if I know Stanley, he'll probably insist on doing that for me, too."

I felt a churning in my stomach and I had to leave Katie's company before I was tempted to swat her. I could feel her eyes following me down the hall and I imagined her gloating with satisfaction.

# 12 ⤳

THE SCIENCE FAIR was taking place at the community building in the city park. Entries from ten surrounding high schools would be included. Hillview's section was to be right in the middle of the building. Kids from other schools were setting up their displays in the booths lined along the sides of the exhibition hall.

Brian Hotchkiss looked warily toward the entries being placed in the section reserved for Wiley K. Bemis High School.

"I got started on mine too late," Brian said. "There's no use entering my contraption." He flourished the tapered metal cylinder he had invented.

"See. Mine isn't the only musical instrument. Someone from Bemis has invented what looks like a piano. Mine will look crummy next to that."

"Everyone can't win," I scolded him. "You have something unusual. You have a place to display it. So there's another musical instrument at the fair. So what?"

"Besides that, I'll have to sit in here and blow the thing all day," Brian grumbled. "Nobody will know what a great range this trombophone has unless I play it."

"Why don't you just put up a sign saying you'll demonstrate it, say, at eleven A.M. and three P.M. only, and then you'll have the rest of the day free," Lee Ann suggested.

"Anyway, I feel kind of guilty, because maybe I thought of the idea of the trombophone, but Stanley practically made the whole outer shell of it in his metal shop."

"Quit worrying," I said. "A lot of these people had some help."

"Where's your exhibit?" Brian asked.

"I was assigned the booth three sections down, and I brought my stuff, but I've decided to withdraw." I had been undecided until just an hour before. "I already got credit for the project as a term report, but it doesn't show up very well. It's just a bunch of charts and graphs and doesn't make a good exhibit among all these jazzy projects with their moving parts. Besides,

Dr. Hummel told me that from a scientific point of view, it wasn't ready. I haven't done enough research on it."

Lee Ann was helping Brian in the trombophone booth. She had made a backdrop with musical notes on it, and a big, glitzy sign done with glitter sprinkled over the letters, announcing the name of the newly invented instrument. She and Brian were putting up this backdrop with masking tape. They had to have it finished by five o'clock, so it would be ready for the opening of the fair the next day.

I went to get my things out of the booth that I'd been assigned. Someone else could use it. It turned out to be right next to Katie Gneiss's.

She was ordering a number of guys around in her cubicle, which centered around a tray of fuzzy, grungy objects, some mushrooms and moldy-looking yucky material. Worse yet, Stanley was crouched down in back of the booth, entangled in a mass of tubes and hoses. Another guy was standing over him putting the finishing touches on a sign that told what the various fungi on the tray were called.

Wanda Zetterquist strolled by with her notepad, making comments for the Hillview *Howl* gossip column. She leaned on my booth and whispered to me. "Just look at Katie," she said. "She had Jeff Hanford collect all those mushrooms, mold, and other disgusting stuff, Al Calkins is doing the sign, and isn't that Stanley Stoneman, your old friend setting up the irrigating system for it? She didn't do one bit of that herself. If she gets any kind of a prize, there's no justice."

I didn't make any comment, but I did look up and down the aisle for Stanley's Paddywhack, which was supposed to be the most sophisticated entry in the science fair and was sure to win first place. I didn't see it. It looked as if he were spending so much time on Katie's exhibit that he hadn't had time to install his own.

"Aren't you entering something? Where's your exhibit?" Wanda asked.

"I did a study on premature babies and how they grow," I said. "But a doctor at the hospital told me I didn't have enough material, so I just decided not to exhibit it."

Katie must have pricked her ears up because she emerged from her booth and strutted in front of mine.

"Did I hear you're taking your entry out?" she asked loudly so that everyone in the vicinity could hear. "Chickening out, eh? Can't take the competition?" She gave a shrill laugh and tossed her head triumphantly toward her booth and its hive of workers.

With that, Stanley popped up from behind the counter where he was fixing the drip system. "You're not withdrawing your project!" he exclaimed as if we had never quarrelled. "Brian warned me you might, but I didn't believe it." He turned and gave Katie a fierce scowl and lurched toward my booth, from which I was scooping up my materials. As he moved, his foot became entangled in a mass of hoses on the floor. Stanley lost his balance and grabbed hold of Katie's fungus tray with one hand, pulling it off its counter. He yanked a tube out of the faucet on the wall and water spurted everywhere.

An outraged screech emerged from Katie. Stanley ignored the wreckage of Katie's fungus collection and when he regained his balance he walked over to confront me. "Meg, don't pull out like this. You worked hard on your project. It's important." He grabbed my arm and twisted me toward him as if we were doing the tango.

Katie stuck her face between Stanley's and mine. "See what she made you do! My exhibit is ruined!" Katie's voice choked with anger. Other exhibitors gathered to watch, and some of them stepped in Katie's fungi.

I tried to shake free of Stanley's grip, but he wouldn't let go. "Your idea was unique. You worked on it for months. Don't give up now."

"Let me go," I yelled. "My exhibit doesn't say what I want it to. I have to have more subjects before it's scientific. I don't want to show it until it's right."

"Listen to me!" Katie's strident voice drowned mine out. "You've wrecked my experiment. You two have pulled down my drip system and knocked over my tray. Just look! All these fungi are mixed together." She glared daggers at Stanley, and I saw one of her helpers sneaking out of her booth. Then she fixed her anger on me. "You made him do this—you destroyed my exhibit because you're jealous of Stanley and me. You don't want to admit that I'm better at science than you are." Katie's face was contorted into a disagreeable expression.

Stanley turned on her with total loathing. "Buzz off, Katie," he said. "Your exhibit was about as scientific as a mud-pie exhibit. It's good riddance."

"I'm telling the fair authorities that you deliberately damaged my display and that Meg Royce put you up to it." Katie returned Stanley's glare. "You're both going to be in hot water."

"Get lost, Gneiss. Meg, let's get out of here." Stanley rushed me out of the booth.

Katie's eyes widened and blazed, not believing that any guy in school could say such a thing to her. She yelled after us as Stanley propelled me toward the exit of the building. "I'm reporting you both. It will be on your record, and you'll both be disqualified." I heard a frustrated squeal ooze from her as we continued walking.

Outside the building Stanley, still gripping my arm, said, "She actually *is* the most irritating person I've ever known." He said it through partially clenched teeth.

"Then why have you been catering to her whims?" I asked, wrenching my arm free, putting some distance between him and me, fixing him with a cold stare that I didn't really mean.

"It's your fault. When you gave me such a bad time, I had to get revenge. I knew nothing would make you so mad as my helping Katie, so I did. You don't need to tell me that it was childish and I was biting off my nose to spite my face. I'm aware of that, so can we drop the subject?"

"My pleasure," I said. "But I'm still disappointed that you did it."

*"You're* disappointed in *me!* How do you think I feel to see you pulling your preemie project out of the fair? Maybe Katie was right, you *are* afraid of the competition."

"Baloney. I never planned on winning anything. And when I showed Dr. Hummel my project and he told me I needed more data, I decided to add babies to it. Maybe it will be in next year's science fair. If it isn't, I'll have a lot of knowledge to start on my career as a pediatrician."

Stanley was silent for a moment. Then he looked at me with a kind of admiration. "That makes sense," he said. "You're starting to sound like a real scientist."

All at once Stanley and I merged together and the past weeks of being apart melted away. He still loved me!

"Meg, I missed you," he said. "I've been miserable."

"Don't ever leave me again, Stanley."

After a bear hug and a few kisses, Stanley held me away as if we were dancing the Lindy and scrutinized me with a delighted smile spreading across his face. "You think your project isn't good enough to enter in the science fair, well, wait till you see what I'm dreaming up now. It puts the Paddywhack in the shade."

"Where is the Paddywhack, anyway? I didn't see it in the fair."

"I haven't unloaded it yet. See, it's in a trailer cart on the back of my car. My booth is all ready for it. All I have to do is set the vehicle in. But, Meg, now that I have you back, I can't wait for you to see the new project I'm working on. Well, listen, why should I describe it to you when you could be seeing it? Come on. Let's take a run out to my lab."

"First, unload your entry. It's almost time for them to close the building for the afternoon."

"There's still time. It only takes five minutes to get to my lab, and you haven't seen my new one yet." Stanley shoved me ahead of him and literally lifted me into his homemade car.

On the way he explained his project, gesturing wildly so that at times I almost had to grab the steering wheel from him. He was at the peak of excitement as we sped away from the park, down the street that led to the Stoneman mansion, and through the gate to the winding driveway that led to his workshop. "Do you know that the United States has more coal than any other country in the world? We don't really need oil here, because we have twenty-seven percent of the world's coal. Only we don't use it, because it pollutes the atmosphere with all this carbon. So I'm making it usable by inventing a gadget that will compress all the smoke from the carbon and keep it from making smog and acid rain."

We pulled up in front of his lab, a low, modern building built over the ruins of the old barn that had been his lab before he blew it up in one of his experiments. He led me in proudly.

"Brian Hotchkiss built his trombophone out here," Stanley said. "It was fun to have him around. It gets lonely, and a guy needs company. But the company I wanted just got here." Stanley took me in his arms again. It was like old times.

"Listen, Meg, about Katie. Let me explain. It was because I was jealous. When I heard that you were going to that ball with one of the Whitlows, I totally cracked up. My mother and dad had tickets to that dance, and I agreed to take DeeDee. I thought that would teach you that you're not the only one who can go out with someone else. Then when she couldn't go, and Katie happened to dial my number, I had this sudden impulse. Bring her, maybe it would make you so furious you'd punch her out, come back to me, and leave the Whitlow guy in the lurch."

"Punch her out! I'm sure! You know you took a real risk. You could have gotten yourself permanently attached to Katie. She was acting like she owned you."

"End of subject. I brought you out here because it's no fun for me to invent stuff unless you can see it." Stanley's eyes blazed. He raked his hand through his hair, rumpling it into an appealing tangle so that I couldn't resist reaching out to cuddle against him. His arms encircled me.

"I'll never be able to do this work without you. Now that you're back with me, I feel my creative juices bubbling."

"I feel like I just came alive, too. While we've been apart, it's been like drifting around in a boat in the middle of a lake without any oars."

"We're never going to be separated again." He gestured at the gadgets around the lab. "A lot of these inventions didn't turn out the way I planned. They were no good because you weren't around my lab."

We were sitting on a bench pushed against the wall, just wallowing in affection and a haze of happiness when suddenly my conscious mind snapped on.

"Stanley!" I exclaimed. "What about your Paddy-whack?" I leapt up and looked out the window. "You don't have any more time. You've got to get that to the fair before it closes. Hurry!"

Stanley pushed his sweater up from his wrist and looked at the time. "It's past five o'clock," he said. "They've closed."

"Maybe if we hurry, there'll still be someone there. They'd let you in late, because your exhibit is supposed to be the star of the show."

"It's too late now, and it doesn't matter, anyway. If your preemie report isn't in, I don't want my entry in either."

"But the Paddywhack deserves to be seen."

"It's already had all the glory it deserves. I've shown

it at NASA and they have pictures of it in their files. I've taken it to three different science fairs around the country. Mr. Grayson has seen it lots of times. It's counted on my grade in both metal shop and physics. What else does it, or I, deserve?

"Besides, if it isn't an entry, anyone could win."

"Maybe they'll put back the fungus collection and Katie will win."

"Not that," Stanley said. "But I'd like to see that Vietnamese kid, Truong somebody, in the running. He devised some kind of fishing gadget which would prevent turtles, dolphins, and pelicans from getting trapped. It's a neat idea that could do a lot of good in the world. Of course, Brian's trombophone was too hastily put together to be in the running."

"But he got credit for having the idea." I reached up and gave him a kiss on the cheek.

A little portable radio was playing on the lab table, and Stanley stood up, pulled me into his arms, and danced me around the lab table.

"So maybe I didn't mix too badly with your friends, after all," he boasted.

"You know what?" I asked as he twirled me. "The summer recreation class is having an advanced ballroom class. I saw it in the catalog."

"You want to join?" Stanley asked, putting his cheek against mine.

"It might be fun. You could go disguised as Richard Linton again. And maybe Kreik and Fancher will be the instructors."

"Who cares? As long as I could dance with you."

Suddenly I had a depressing thought. "After this summer I won't see you anymore. You'll be off at school three thousand miles away. You were accepted, weren't you?" He nodded. I crept closer to him and he pulled his arm tighter around me until my head was on his shoulder.

"That's not going to happen, now that I have you back. Didn't we just promise never to leave each other?"

"But I thought MIT was your lifetime goal."

"I was also accepted at Stanford, a great engineering school, and closer to a certain person."

"Right next door, practically," I said. "But if that certain person is who I think it is, she might not want to influence your decision. She wants you to have the best for your fantastic inventiveness."

"All the profs at both schools are tops," Stanley said. "The thing that will make the difference between them is having you within inspiring distance."

My heart almost exploded when he said that. I thought maybe I saw Mrs. Stoneman looking out the second floor window and was happy that Stanley and I were back together again.

"Let's definitely sign up for advanced ballroom," I said.

His eyes flashed with new and exciting creative sparks. He twirled me in an arch turn. "Good idea," he said.

# About the Author

Well traveled and an avid bird watcher, Emily Hallin is the author of more than twenty-five Young-Adult books. The only girl among four boys, she grew up in Colorado, then later moved to Missouri, where she attended the state university. In later years she worked at Stanford University, where she came into contact with many young people who have inspired her work. Ms. Hallin is the author of three books about Meg and Stanley: *Partners, Changes,* and *Risks,* all available in Archway Paperbacks.